THE HONORABLE HITMAN

A.J Turton

First published 2025
by Rowanvale Books Ltd
The Gate
Keppoch Street
Roath
Cardiff
CF24 3JW
www.rowanvalebooks.com

A CIP catalogue record for this book is available from the British Library.
ISBN: 978-1-83584-074-0
eBook ISBN: 978-1-83584-073-3

This book owes its birth to many people: my wife Becky whose encouragement and support have been unwavering; my daughter Sophie who loved my stories as a child, and as an adult enrolled me in writing workshops to sharpen my skills; long-time friends David Wragg and Mick Catherall, who provided valuable advice as the story evolved, and all the people I've met whose quirks and idiosyncrasies fed my imagination and seeped into the characters I've created. And of course, thanks to the Rowanvale Books team – they have been wonderful to work with.

"Fiction is the lie through which we tell the truth."
Albert Camus

PROLOGUE

I've killed one hundred and thirteen people since I turned eighteen, one hundred and eleven men and two women. One hundred and twelve went quick and easy, one clean shot each –would barely have known their time had come. One died sobbing and pleading – the last one.

I served my country well, never questioned the rightness of what I did. I killed our enemies and kept the country safe. And I was proud of my service. Proud of what it said about how I was raised and the hometown that shaped me.

I got medals and awards for the one hundred and twelve kills my government ordered me to make. There will be no accolades this time, though – they didn't sanction the last one, even though it was the most righteous kill of them all. No question.

PART ONE

CHAPTER ONE

It's eight years since the last logs were cut and the mill closed, but the air is still rich with the sweet vanilla scent of fresh-cut white oak. Every day, Dad came home soaked with sweat, but he always smelled good – the scent clung to him like it clung to everything else in Oakvale. I loved that smell.

Oakvale was pretty then. Well-tended, red-tile-roofed homes tightly clustered around the square and dotting the gentle slope down to the river. Its streets bustled with the energy of small-town life. Now, from my perch in the old mill's roof space, it looks miserable and bleak – dilapidated homes, gardens overgrown, the forest crowding it out. Everyone gone.

The river still runs fast past the mill. Back in the day, every day except Sunday, it was packed with barges carrying our timber to the city. Oakvale was a confident town, sure of its place in the world. Not a wealthy place, but rich with pride – pride in the town we'd built, pride in our independence, pride in a hard day's work well done. A tight-knit, hardworking community. The big joke back then was we had a police officer, John Betts, but there was no crime. We liked John, but we resented paying for him. Resented the government for making us.

Things changed slowly at first. Fewer orders at the mill, Mom making things go a little further at the dinner table, kids wearing the same clothes for longer. Bit by bit the town was dying around us, we just didn't see it. Then the mill closed. Everything in Oakvale depended on it – we never expected or wanted to know anything else – but when the mill closed it killed the town. Gradually, reluctantly, people moved away. Those who stayed fill the town's cemetery.

They'll look for me here, of course. Black Ops know people on the run hole up where they feel safe – often their hometown. But they know I'm good, so most will assume I'd be too smart to come back here. They'll have a quick look around, tick that box and move on. They'll be back when all other leads grow cold, but by then I'll be gone.

The mill's roof space provides clear views in every direction. Clean shots too, although I don't plan to take any.

A flicker of movement – I swing my rifle up, nestle it snugly into my shoulder, let out a slow breath and focus through the sight, keeping my right index finger away from the trigger. The only road into town is empty, but dirt flicks out from behind what used to be Mrs. Johnson's garden wall. Pecking at the dirt, skinny chickens shuffle out.

I lower my rifle and wait. I need them to come, look around and leave, then I can do what I came home for.

CHAPTER TWO

It can be a long wait for the moment to arrive – but not this time. The wind carries the rumble of diesel engines into town long before two armored troop carriers growl over the hill and chug down the slope into the main square, the sun glinting off their polished metal frames. Soldiers jump out, split into units and move into each quarter of the town at the double. I don't recognize any of them, but they all have a familiar look – fresh-faced kids straight out of bootcamp. Like I said, Black Ops don't expect to find me here. They've sent kids for the experience. Just ticking a box, something to tell the politicians baying for my blood: *He's not in Oakvale.*

Two minutes after they disembarked, a pair of jogging footfalls come to a halt at the mill's heavy oak entrance door. Two young voices filter up through the rafters.

"It's the perfect place," says one, eagerly. "It's the tallest building in town, an excellent place to snipe from. He can see everything that's going on, and with 'condemned' signs all over it, most won't take even a quick look inside; he'll think he won't be disturbed if he's hiding here."

I nod approvingly – ten out of ten. *Well done, young man!*

As the factory door groans open, a laughing second voice says, "Looks spooky. Better not be any ghosts!"

No ghosts here, just plenty of cobwebs and dust accumulated over the eight years since the mill shut down for good. And no signs of me; I climbed up the back of the building and entered through the roof hatch where the wood used to be winched down and loaded onto the barges. I'm relaxed, confident that they won't venture into the rafters.

"If he's here, he'll be high up where he's got a view," the second soldier says, stifling a dust-fueled cough. "But we should do this like we trained, right? Clear one floor at a time, bottom up. Left first, then right, alternate who goes in and who backs up. Clear this floor then move up."

I silently applaud their plan as metallic clicks tell me they've cocked their weapons. In my mind's eye, I watch them systematically move along the spine of the building, opening doors, entering fast with aggression, finding nothing then moving on.

Fifteen minutes later, they're back in the lobby.

"Next floor then," soldier one says.

But a shrill whistle cuts the air; their search is over, like it is for the other soldiers spread around the town. As I expected, just a cursory look and then move on.

I watch the troop carriers leave, wait ten minutes, then, seeing no activity, check that my rucksack is securely hidden and head out and across the square towards the black-slate-roofed church.

CHAPTER THREE

Oakvale's cemetery is like most others: dismal, soaked in the sadness of loss and littered with stained, bent headstones, the intention to maintain them buried under busy lives moving relentlessly forward. But Oakvale's cemetery is different in one important way – my parents are here. They lie side by side at the end of the last row, at the bottom of the slope, separated from the river only by the thick hawthorn hedge.

I sit on the green, wooden bench I placed under the weeping willow and try to gather my thoughts. Focus is hard to find; being with them again brings back so many memories.

I turned out to be an only child, so Mom and Dad poured into me the hopes and dreams they'd built for what should have been a house-full of kids. They believed in The Dream – work hard and you can do anything you want, be anyone you want to be. So, I set my sights on becoming a doctor. I never dreamed I'd end up looking down the sight of a gun; taking lives, not saving them.

The winds that sweep down from the mountains into the valley are fiercest in winter but sometimes they send a chill even now in early spring. The willow's branches twist under a sudden gust, and my hair, long and dirty from my last mission, whips across my face.

Just before I turned ten, powerful winter winds toppled two ancient oaks set slightly apart from the forest at the end of our street. I watched in awe as Dad set upon the fallen trees with an axe, tearing into them, dripping with sweat although it was a frigid day. He had a smile on his face, the glint in his eye never wavering. I found out why on my tenth birthday – from the fallen giants he'd made a solid oak desk and a chair, a place for me to study, to fulfill my dreams. I loved that desk and chair, hewn by my dad's skills from wood nourished and grown in the soil under my feet – the same soil all Oakvalers were rooted in.

The desk felt exactly right from the moment I first sat at it. I placed it under the single-pane window at the end of my bedroom, facing the river and overlooking the town. I sat at that desk every night for the next seven years, my feet warmed by Mom's multi-colored, hand-woven, woolen rug. And as the sounds of the day ebbed away, lights went on in living rooms and smoke from freshly lit wood fires drifted across town, I studied.

I loved those days, and I loved learning. Math and Chemistry were my favorites. I loved the challenging work. I loved the community I was part of, where everyone knew everyone, and everyone wanted me to succeed. Life was good.

The gravel on the canal-side path crunches behind me. Trained responses take over. I throw myself forward onto the grass and crawl at an angle to the churchyard gate, which opens onto the path, to get a clear view left and right. There's no one there, just a broken branch shaken loose by the wind and smashed on the path's granite slabs.

I brush myself down and sit up again. There were times when the path was full of people chattering optimistically about their futures; then the mill failed, the money dried up and everyone's lives changed. Mom and Dad had to use the money they'd saved for my college to keep a roof over our heads and food on the table, and I needed to help pay the bills – college would have to wait.

There were no jobs in Oakvale, though, and becoming a doctor seemed like a faint hope, so I followed my school buddies into the army. It was the right thing to do for our family back then, and I was glad to do it. I was disappointed about college, but not bitter; if I couldn't be a doctor, I'd make a difference some other way.

Mom and Dad were so proud of me for showing the right attitude and getting on with things even when my plans were in tatters. They were proud of me for all the medals I won, too. But now, as I look over at their granite headstones, an image as clear as day comes to my mind's eye: they're sitting upright in their chairs at our old kitchen table, like we're all together again, a family discussing the important issues of the day. This time, though, they look sad and disappointed, and it hurts.

Dad says, "I just don't get it, son. We've always been so proud of you… but this?! How could you?"

A gentle rain begins to sprinkle the cemetery, making damp my already dirty hair.

"That bastard had it coming," I growl then immediately stop myself. Too defensive. Too loud.

I stand up, the rain dripping off my hair as I bow my head, clasp my hands in front of me and breathe deeply. Then I try again, softer and more carefully this time.

"I understand you're angry, Dad, and I am sorry for that. But he betrayed us all, and that couldn't go unpunished. He told us what we wanted to hear, gave us hope. Told us that Oakvale and all the other places like it would thrive again. It's why you stayed. You'd be alive now if you'd moved out when the rest of us did."

The words burn in my throat. They both look hurt, and I see Dad itching to correct me; he always said, "if onlys" and "what ifs" are pointless, self-indulgent. I take another deep breath and search for an even keel.

"But I understand. I do. Once he'd ignited the flame of hope, you just couldn't let go of it. And he knew that. He played with your hope like a toy, just like he played with the lives of the millions who believed in him. They wanted to swagger down the streets again, heads held high, feeling like winners, and he promised them they would."

I swallow hard and fight the rage that burns whenever I think about his manipulation – so many good people taken for fools.

"But when re-born hope turns to dust it's worse than having no hope at all. Right, Dad? Right, Mom?" They both nod reluctantly, so I continue, "Nothing actually changed one iota; even his rhetoric didn't change – it was like, if he said it everyone would believe it, despite the evidence of their own eyes! But if we were on top again, like he always claimed, it certainly wasn't happening here. And the disappointment crushed you. *He crushed you.*"

I sit down again and lean towards them before continuing, gently now as I see their shoulders sag in recognition of the brutal truth.

"He had to pay; you taught me that. An eye for an eye. What happened was simply justice. He got what he deserved."

They silently stare back at me, pain etched across their faces, then give a small nod in acceptance. It's as much as I can hope for.

CHAPTER FOUR

As the cemetery's black metal gate clicks shut behind me, another gust of wind whips up off the river. I pull my heavy, sand-colored wool coat tight around me and head towards the mill along the tow path.

I stop dead after a few steps, glimpsing movement and color through the overgrown holly bush that marks the end of the churchyard and the start of the town square. Soundlessly, I move close to the bush and peer through the gaps between its prickly leaves. Three people. All civilians. No threat, but sloppy of me not to register their arrival; a sign I need to rest. The twenty-four intense, adrenalin-fueled hours since his death have taken a toll.

"I didn't realize that literally everyone was gone from this place, Jess. Sorry for that," says a heavy-set, mid-forties man with wiry, salt and pepper hair and a voice that squeaks like it never broke properly. "It would have been great to hear from people who knew him, for sure, but we're here now so let's just wander around, see if we can get a sense of the place that made him. Can't hurt and might help, right?"

Journalists. *Very* sloppy of me. I should have expected the press to come. Even though I've spent most of the last eight years in the desert, I know well enough how fast they work.

An athletic-looking woman dressed in black leggings, a white T-shirt and blue gilet – presumably Jess – nods and turns to a stocky, plain, younger woman weighed down with cameras and equipment. "Be ready to roll, Sylvie, just in case."

There's no time or place for me to hide. If I could slip quietly into the river, I could hold my breath long enough to reach the mill – the current's strong enough to carry me there quickly – but there's no way to do that, nor to burrow into the hedge, without alerting them – they're too close.

I turn on my heel and walk hurriedly back towards the cemetery, hoping they'll stay in the square or climb the hill away from the river. But, they head for the tow path.

I'm almost at the cemetery gate when I hear a woman's voice: "Oh wow, someone *is* here!" Then, shouting after me, "Excuse me, sir. SIR, please wait!"

Head down, I slowly turn to face her, weighing up my options as I move. None are good. Run, and they'll know something's wrong, maybe alert the forces, bring them back before I'm ready; pretend I don't hear, and she'll come closer and ask again; and hurting them is not an option – they've done nothing to deserve it. But, if they recognize me, I'm in trouble.

I walk slowly back, keeping my head down and watching her through my eyebrows.

Jess is in her early thirties, attractive but with a tired, haunted look – striving to make a career for herself in a cutthroat industry, I assume. Her jaw is set strong; she looks like a fighter. I like that.

Jess jogs the last few steps towards me, fixing me with a frank, appraising stare. Her hazel eyes are warm and kind. Up close, I feel like we've met before although I can't place where or when. The frisson of connection as I take her outstretched hand is powerful.

Sylvie, weighed down by her gear, and the older guy, out of breath from the modest exercise, catch up. Sylvie lifts her camera, and I instinctively raise my hand to stop her filming, but immediately relax – the man reflected in her lens is tanned with matted blond hair down to his shoulders, a thick, greasy beard, and clothes stained with sweat and crusted with dirt. I'm wearing the outcome of weeks undercover in the desert. I hardly recognize myself – there's every chance they won't either.

"Thank you." Jess's eyes tell me she felt the connection, too. "Have we met?" she asks, genuine and friendly. "You look kind of familiar."

I shake my head.

She smiles again, a little shyly this time, shrugs and pulls a photo out of her inside-jacket pocket. I hold my breath.

"We're just looking for people who know this guy: David Smith. The army is giving us very little. Just bare bones. It's like he didn't even exist before yesterday."

I force a neutral expression, but I understand. Governments like plausible deniability –people with jobs like mine don't officially exist. They haven't even released my real name.

"Anyway, what we got from the army's statement was he grew up around here," Jess continues, "so we thought we'd see what we could find, maybe meet some people who knew him. Maybe you did?" she says hopefully, encouraging me to take the photo.

I glance at it. It's me, of course, but me eight years ago – fresh-faced, neat, trim, polished. Eyes shining with the zeal of youth. I liked being that young man, wish I could turn the clock back.

I say nothing, so Jess fills the gap: "Only, we're real keen to learn something about him. You know, after what he did. Get the backstory, kind of thing."

I nod. "Of course, yeah, I get it. But I can't help, I'm afraid. I'm just passing through." I turn to walk away.

Jess trots to catch up and falls into step alongside me. "Well, maybe there's someone else in town who could help?"

"Doubt it. Place looks like it's been deserted for years."

"Right, right," Jess says, grabbing my arm to slow me down.

Training kicks in again, and I instinctively turn square-on to her, ready to fight. I see fear flash in her eyes.

"S-s-sorry, sorry," she says, taking a backward step before quickly regaining her composure. "What did you say your name was again?"

"I'm just a guy who likes to keep to himself," I say and turn away again, but Jess grabs my hand – brave after my initial re-action – shakes it with muttered thanks and leaves a card in my palm.

"Well, thanks again," she says. "And if anything comes back to you, just give me a call, okay?"

I like her determination and can't help smiling. Nodding, I slip the card into my pocket and force myself not to look back as I head towards the mill. I feel her eyes on me all the way.

CHAPTER FIVE

Jess and her crew were the first but they won't be the last media to head into Oakvale, and I'm not ready. Snipers plan carefully, and I'm good at it. Very good. I plan weeks ahead, and every angle has been considered by the time I act. Number one hundred thirteen was not planned, though, and it was messy. And now I'm scrambling in unfamiliar territory – the hunted not the hunter.

I need a quiet space to gather my thoughts. I grab my rucksack from the mill and head into the woods, taking the westerly path, which emerges at the top of John's Hill.

John Betts's former home sits alone at the hill's bottom; it's only three-quarters of a mile from town, and the walk through the woods is pleasant, but his home was placed there to make a point: we don't need a policeman, even if the government thinks we do. So, we provided him with a simple A-frame bungalow, separate from the town. Just two bedrooms at the rear, and a kitchen and living room at the front, symmetrically split either side of a hallway running from the front to the back door, all topped with a tin roof. The townsfolk regretted it when we got to know John; it was harsh of us to treat him like that. But he took it in his stride and made a home of it – painted the exterior walls white, the roof red and its doors and window casements black, and he planted and harvested his crops just like us. By the time the mill failed, he took its failure as badly as any of us. Oakvale had a way of doing that; eventually every newcomer sank their roots into its rich soil, just like those of us born there.

I approach the house carefully, but there are no signs of life. I find the spare key where John always used to leave it, on a hook at the back of the woodshed he built. I let myself into the kitchen to find John's pots, pans, plates, cutlery and unopened cans carefully arranged, the beds made and cut logs by the fire. If it wasn't for the thick layer of dust, I'd suppose John had just stepped out and would be back any minute. Truth is, when he left, he probably hoped he would, too.

I open John's attic door and carefully place my rucksack out of sight; what I have in there must only see the light of day when the time's right. I then spend the next hour securing the perimeter close to the house and up the hill.

After helping myself to a can of John's beans and a cup of his coffee, I sink into his old, leather armchair and look up the hill towards the woods. I need to think through my next moves carefully.

But I'm asleep before a single coherent thought forms.

CHAPTER SIX

I wake with a start, instantly alert. I'm unsure how long I've slept, but the evening is closing in, swallowing the daylight. I hear walkie-talkie chatter, distant but unmistakably military – presumably what woke me. I run though the standard fugitive search protocol: first, check the target's hometown; next, check close associates; then other places of personal significance. There's no way the rookies could have done all of that yet.

Then the penny drops. The rookies will still be actively searching, logical step by logical step, keeping the media occupied with briefings along the way and providing a cover for the government's real intentions. The team in the woods are not rookies; they're Black Ops. I shouldn't be surprised – the government doesn't want me to stand trial, they won't give me a platform to tell the world why I did what I did. They need me to disappear.

A Black Ops team is here to take me out.

My pulse races, but my mind is clear like it always is when I'm on an assignment. Keeping to the room's growing shadows, I crawl into the hallway then run at a crouch out of the back door and into the tree line. I move quickly uphill as the thick, musty forest invades my senses.

A walkie-talkie crackles again, maybe a hundred and fifty feet away, still deep in the woods but moving towards the ridge above John's house. They'll be fanning out now, moving towards the forest edge, hyper-alert; they'll process any movement and be ready to fire in less than a second. And they'll squeeze the trigger if it's me in their sights; their orders will be simple and unambiguous – shoot on sight.

I lean against a thick poplar two feet inside the wood, facing the valley. John's house is in full view at the bottom of the hill. I steady my breathing and wipe away the sweat now streaming down my face. The platoon is moving as stealthily as it can, but last autumn's twigs and desiccated leaves rustle and snap under their feet. They're a hundred feet from the ridge. Faint voices left and right confirm that they're moving in a single line.

I scan the valley again. Near the top, five yards below the tree line, eight metal spikes linked by a thin wire are just visible. Beyond them, it's three hundred yards of open space to the house. Looking up, I notice that spring's rebirth has created a canopy thick enough to hide the darkening sky. And if it can hide the sky, it can hide me. I crouch, spring and grab the lowest branch, then swing my legs over its bough. A flock of birds races from the tree, cawing loudly, spreading alarm until a cacophony fills the forest. It's over in seconds, but it's enough time for me to find a place in the canopy unheard – invisible and cocooned in the poplar's sweet honey smell.

The voices are now close enough for me to recognize. Sergeant Garverich, from the group I trained with, speaks in a loud whisper to the troops gathered either side of him:

"If he's here he'll be in the house. We'll rush him, take him down fast; maximum speed, maximum aggression. There's twenty of us and one of him, but don't fire until he fires – if he's not here he'll be in the town proper, and we don't want to alert him. But, if he does shoot, open fire with everything you've got, okay?"

No one responds, but the obvious question hangs in the air, so Garverich continues, "Don't worry about getting hit, lads. I know we'll be exposed, but our body armor will do its job. Trust me, we'll be fine."

He has not thought it through. I *know* they have body armor. I *know* that my bullets won't stop them. He should have asked himself what else I might do if I'd chosen John's house as a base. But he always preferred action to analysis.

A radio bursts into life. I hold my breath while Garverich shares his plan with Black Ops HQ. The call ends quickly. Decision made.

"We're on, lads," he says, his voice thick with excitement. "We go in ten."

As Garverich counts down, I smile grimly and carefully shimmy behind the tree's trunk, placing it between me and the house. It's good cover but with a clear view of the slope they'll head down.

I slow my breathing.

Holding their tight line, they start to move quickly down the hillside, weapons ready but silent.

I count: one second... two seconds... three... four... five... six... seven... eight...

Garverich should have realized something was wrong by now. No shots from the house, no signs of life. He should have brought them to a halt. But he didn't. He always let emotion cloud his judgment. His biggest failing.

They're a foot from the wire now. The wire connecting eight mines across the width of the hillside. The mines I planted when I chose John's house as my base.

I duck behind the trunk as the first explosion cracks the air, quickly followed by seven more – fast, brutal, efficient. Then, silence.

I peer out. Nothing moves. The acrid smell of explosives mixed with death hangs in the air, crushing the sweet smells of spring's new life.

Surveying my grizzly handiwork is necessary; good tradecraft demands no loose ends. But it comes at a cost. Every life I've taken squats on my soul, chewing up the best of me bit by bit. Except number one hundred thirteen.

CHAPTER SEVEN

Making good choices under pressure is the difference between winning a fight and being buried in a ditch with a bullet in the head. I must move fast now – when Garverich fails to make contact, a second Black Ops team will be dispatched. They'll know by now that something's wrong.

As I jog back to collect my rucksack from John's, I consider my options. None are good. I have no plans; I'm scrambling, and my pursuers do this for a living. Anxiety bites at my stomach. All Black Ops' advantages race through my head, then a glimmer of an idea shows itself dimly in the shadows of my mind. Wiping the sweat from my eyes, I concentrate hard and slowly bring it into focus: Black Ops work undercover, unseen. The nature of their work demands it; their actions need deniability, so the light of public scrutiny is always to be avoided. I need to force them into the light, force them out of their comfort zone.

As the thought forms, I quickly grow comfortable with it. I know from my brush with the journalists that my current, tramp-like appearance can help me – people avoid tramps, and I'm not easy to recognize from the photo the army released. It's risky, but

I decide to head into the city, to a busy place, a place where Black Ops would never tread, somewhere I can hunker down for a short while and plan my next steps. But Basin Lake is ninety minutes by car. I need transport.

I know without checking that John's place has nothing for me; John never owned a vehicle, he walked everywhere, or else he rode his bicycle around the town. But I remember the mill owned two trucks. It's a long shot, but it's the first place to check.

The light's fading fast when I reach the mill, and the town is deathly quiet. It's hot and sticky, and I'm dripping sweat. I slip my rucksack off, break the loading bay door lock with a rock and slide the heavy barriers open – no need to cover my tracks any longer.

I scan the space with my flashlight. The smell of oil is still strong, but the bay is empty. Faded tire tracks are the only sign that trucks ever used the place. The second Black Ops team will already be in the air by now. Bile bites at my throat, and my mind wildly races without direction up one cul-de-sac after another.

Sometimes in life, thoughts arrive out of nowhere – not the result of focused, logical thought, just suddenly there and demanding attention. The thought that lands now makes my stomach churn, but if it proves out, I'll be on my way.

CHAPTER EIGHT

The tangle of charred wood, metal and brick is unmissable. On the right-hand side of Pinebark Avenue, halfway down, is all that's left of the life Mom and Dad built.

The investigators said it was a chimney fire that spread quickly. When money got low and they ran out of seasoned wood, Mom and Dad took to burning their furniture when the weather turned bitter. The chimney lining wasn't built for that. Apparently, the house was ablaze in minutes, impossible for the fire service to contain.

I was in the desert when it happened, to kill another "enemy of the state" on One Hundred and Thirteen's orders. I didn't know about the fire until a month later, or that it had taken my mom and dad. I was furious – apparently the mission was too important and had to continue regardless, so they'd chosen not to tell me. That order had come directly from One Hundred and Thirteen.

I missed their funeral, too, because of that decision. Even when I got back to home base I was only in the country for a week before my final sanctioned mission took me to the Middle

East again. I visited Mom and Dad's graves and built the bench under the willow before I left, but I didn't visit the house, didn't want my childhood memories charred at the edges. Now I have no choice.

I avoid looking at what's left of our old home and head straight towards the garage that stands a few feet from the house, off-set to the right-hand side. It's blackened by the flames but it's still standing. My excitement grows. I jog into the garden and head for the rear of the garage where Dad assembled a simple lean-to, which he used as a workspace – a metal frame covered by rigid sheets of corrugated plastic, the place he happily spent hours creating whatever pieces of furniture he thought we needed.

The lean-to is bent and buckled by the heat, but I manage to swing open the unlocked door. The room looks just as I remember it, lined with shelves crowded with tools and engine parts that might one day find a use. Against the back wall is Dad's work bench, a chipped, blue-painted vice jutting out from its edge and his rusted metal toolbox at its center.

I stop for a moment and take a deep breath. His smell is still here, faint and mixed with tool oil but unmistakably him. Tears well up, but I swallow them down and focus.

Standing in the center of the room is what I've come for: the cheap, no frills, red Honda motorcycle I bought when I passed my driving test. I'm relieved but sad, too – I'd barely had a chance to use it before I joined up, and when I left, I told Mom and Dad to sell it and use the money. If they'd done that and bought coal instead of burning their furniture, maybe things would have worked out differently.

Forcing the thought away, I fish out the bike's key from Dad's toolbox – exactly where I left it – which probably means the engine hasn't been turned over since I left. Anxiety claws at my gut again, fear that it won't start.

I dust down the old machine and wheel it into the backyard. I smear the registration plates with mud – blurring the images that I assume CCTV will capture as I ride into the city – and check the bike over. The tires are in good shape, and it feels good to sit on its still-shiny black leather seat again.

It starts on the third try.

CHAPTER NINE

A troop plane passes overhead, descending towards Oakvale as I join the freeway – the replacement Black Ops crew, I assume. Even in the fading light they'll be scanning the area, looking for anything out of the ordinary, anything that could give me away. Adrenalin floods my system, but I force myself to put my sadness and anger aside – they are distractions I can't afford. I keep a consistent speed and focus on the road ahead.

It's raining steadily. The road is slick; the earthy smell of fresh rainfall rises from it and invades my nostrils. I need to concentrate hard to maintain my pace; my head-start is negligible and the urge to speed is strong. It won't take them long to discover I'm gone and then they'll quickly move on again. I need to focus everything on my next steps.

Traffic's sparse on the 201 into Basin Lake, and the nine miles from the city limits to the lake's shoreline are flat and depressing, matching the drizzle and darkening sky. Tired homes are clustered around stripped-down factories whose role in supplying the world's automobiles ended a decade ago.

Like Oakvale's mill, the once grand factories stand as a grim reminder of a failed manufacturing past. But, unlike in Oakvale, local entrepreneurs have made a start on their own regeneration instead of waiting for politicians like One Hundred and Thirteen to keep their bloated promises. Signs on factory fronts advertise everything from Yoga classes to custom-built furniture, auto repairs to cupcake manufacture – small businesses doing their best to keep Basin Lake alive. Their resilience makes me smile. These people are what our country is all about; they're the kind of people I killed others to protect. They deserve a better return than the politicians have given them, especially One Hundred and Thirteen.

Freedom Square sits on the lakeside, its vast flagstone space bordered on either side by office towers connected by a shopping mall, which faces the deep, slate-gray lake. A steady stream of workers trickles from the offices into the square. The rain is heavy now, and it's almost dark.

I leave the bike in a quiet corner of a parking lot and turn my back to the CCTV cameras as I take off my helmet and pull up my jacket hood. I strap my rucksack on and ascend the stairs to the square, looking down whenever I pass someone.

I emerge next to the granite Loaves and Fishes Presbyterian Church, which stands sentinel on the lakeside. Its spire doubles as a lighthouse, and the light is flashing its regular, even signal – nothing to worry about tonight. At least, not so far. But Basin Lake rapidly gets dangerous when the weather worsens – rip tides develop, and when the north wind blows, vessels that get caught in them can quickly hit trouble. Many a fishing boat has been lost to their brutal power.

I force myself to walk unhurriedly towards the green Baxter's coffee chain sign. I know I'm not easy to identify at the moment but, even so, I discretely scan for any signs of unwanted interest as I join the line to place my order. There are none – direct from the desert and with the appearance of a vagrant, I look nothing like the fresh-faced recruit on the front pages of the papers strewn across the tables and on the TV behind the counter, broadcasting the early evening news.

The middle-aged couple ahead of me order complicated-sounding coffees and argue about whether oat milk or full fat gives the best cappuccino froth. Their banality is a welcome distraction. I relax a little.

With a white Styrofoam cup of black coffee, a plastic bottle of spring water and the last ham and cheese sandwich, I sit at a table at the café's rear with my back to the wall and a clear view of the door. I tuck my rucksack behind my legs as I continue to scan my surroundings. The low hum of conversation fills the almost-full café; no one is paying attention to the animated TV news anchor's description of One Hundred and Thirteen's death, and no one gives me a second glance. At least for a short while, I can hide in plain sight while I figure out my next move.

The coffee is bitter, and the burnt taste makes me grimace, but it gives me a jolt and clears my head. I lean back in my seat and bite into the sandwich as a newsflash cuts across the anchor's presentation.

My mouth is suddenly too dry to chew – a time-stamped image of me entering the freeway fills the screen. It's taken from behind, so my face is hidden, but despite my efforts, the bike's number plate is easy to read; I didn't think about the rain washing off the mud. Black Ops must have found Garverich and scoured the footage from traffic cameras along the route.

A number to call if the bike is seen scrolls across the screen. There's a reward for information leading to my capture. They've upped the ante and bought the public into the hunt – but if a call comes in, I know they will still try to take me out discreetly, away from public view.

I feel suddenly claustrophobic. Black Ops are relentless, and the pressure on them to eliminate me will grow with every hour I'm free. I obviously can't use the Honda again, and, even though they don't seem to have an image of my current appearance, I can't risk staying in the café.

Keeping my head down as I exit, I walk as naturally as I can towards the lakeshore, glad at least that the rain has stopped. Passing a group of women animatedly discussing One Hundred and Thirteen's death, I recognize one of the voices and half-turn, catching sight of Jess, the reporter, as the café door closes behind her. She doesn't see me.

Suddenly heavy with weariness, I head to the Liberation Woods entrance, immediately east of Freedom Square, in search of a safe place to sleep away from prying eyes. The woods comprise a hundred acres of protected temperate hardwood forest, the city's nod to the area's wilderness history. Once in the woods, I head towards an outcrop of basalt rocks that interrupts the forest's flow about a mile from the square. I used to play there as a kid when Mom and Dad made their twice-yearly trips to the city in search of new clothes. The deal was that I could play at the rock – and avoid the boredom of traipsing round the stores – as long as I met them outside McGilvery's burger bar at the time they specified. And to make sure I didn't waver, they promised me a soft serve to follow my burger and fries if I was there on time. That was more than enough incentive for me back then. I was never late. Not once!

I'm still smiling at the memory as I come into the clearing around the rock and take in its grandeur again. Facing me is sheer basalt that rises about fifty feet, jutting above the surrounding treetops. From its peak, the rock tapers down along a distance of seventy feet to only one foot above the ground at the other end, making it easy to walk from ground level to the top and its views of the woods and the city's distant skyline. The surface of the rock has been worn smooth by tourists, but its sides remain rugged and hard, pitted with holes worn into it by centuries of freezing and unfreezing, cracking away chunks of the hard stone.

A full moon shines through the treetops, and I spot a crawl space at the base of the long side of the rock, facing away from the lake. I wriggle inside the rock with my rucksack behind me. I'm asleep in seconds.

CHAPTER TEN

The crunching sound registers moments before the burning pain in my jaw rocks me sideways. I'm on my feet as my attacker's boot swings in again. I grab it and run forward, tipping my assailant onto his back. I follow him down, smashing his nose with my right fist and pressing my left forearm across his throat. His breath comes in rasps. Someone grabs me round the neck and pulls my dog tags tight, strangling me. The chain snaps, and the second attacker falls backwards. I'm on my feet again in an instant, ready to strike.

The overwhelming smell of booze stops me.

"Don't hurt me, okay. I'm sorry, *we're* sorry. Right, Greg?!" The second assailant is yelping and looking pleadingly at his buddy who's bent double, puking.

Kids! Teenagers, by the look of them, out for a night's camping and boozing away from their parents' eyes.

My jaw's swelling, but when I touch it, there's no sign of blood.

"You better let us go, mister," the one who kicked me squeals, his voice quivering. "My dad's Chief of Police for this whole county and he'll string you up for what you just did." He holds up his mobile in front of his face and taps at it angrily. "I'm calling my dad right now."

I know there's no signal this deep into the forest so I do nothing to stop him. I'm seething though.

My anger must show on my face because the boy continues, "Chief Nichols. Remember that name, asshole, he'll—"

I kick him in the guts before he can finish the sentence. He rolls over and pukes again.

I don't need to commit Chief Nichols's name to memory; I already know who he is. He was John Betts's boss. John called him "ironsides" because he was so rigid. Everything for him was black or white, right or wrong – nothing in between. I used to see him in Oakvale from time to time, his back ramrod straight and with an angry scowl on his face as he strutted around town with John at his side. As the thought settles, my anger dissipates – there's always more to it than meets the eye when kids act out, especially with a parent like Nichols. I decide to give them a break.

"Get out of here while you still can," I snarl, then lunge forward scarily enough for them to jump up and run.

Once they're gone, I wash my face at the lakeshore and assess the damage. Certain that nothing is broken, I check that my rucksack hasn't been tampered with, haul it onto my back and take a slow walk along the lakeside path back to town, my jaw throbbing.

CHAPTER ELEVEN

When I reach Basin Lake, there's a commotion in the square – about thirty uniformed policemen, armed and wearing protective gear. To avoid attention, I keep my head down and hold an easy pace as I head towards Baxter's.

I'm pulling on the door handle when a voice behind me stops me in my tracks.

"Don't go in, Frankie. It's not safe."

Hearing my real name jolts me and, despite myself, I spin around to see who's talking – not cool, definitely a movement anyone watching would notice.

Jess continues before I can speak, "Those two boys you 'met', well, one took a photo of you, and it's all already all over the news." An image of the chief's son claiming to call his dad comes back to me; he must have taken the photo then. "And the other kid got your dog tags. The chief used his contacts to get your real ID, and it's all over the news, too."

I reach for my neck and then remember the chain snapped when the kid tried to strangle me. He must have held on to them. Both boys were smarter than I thought. Again, I'm aware of how far out of my comfort zone I am – the prey instead of the predator. I don't know how to play this role. I need to sharpen up fast.

As if reading my thoughts, Jess smiles. "The police immediately mounted a search party; they'll be heading into the woods any minute."

"Just the police? No army?"

Jess nods. "As far as anyone knows."

I knew then that I'd got lucky that morning – Jess realizes it, too. Black Ops must already be in the woods, targeting a quick ending. There's no way they'd allow the police to take me. The government will not want a trial; they will not want what I know about One Hundred and Thirteen to make the news. On the other hand, the appearance of a good faith effort by the police to capture me is useful cover for them.

Jess glances across the square then takes my hand, turning away, pulling me with her. "We need to move," she says.

I hesitate – I can't put her in danger.

She turns back, a puzzled frown clouding her face that is quickly replaced with a smile. "Come on, Frankie. You really don't remember do you? Eight years old, summer camp on the lakeshore? I felt like I knew you back in Oakvale, but the David Smith name didn't fit and you look so different, but then they used your real name this morning and everything clicked."

Foggy memories come back to me of a gloriously hot summer on the lake, and a little girl who was gutsy and quick and good at every sport, so much so that I always wanted to be on her side.

"Jess! That Jess. Yes, I do remember, sorry!"

"That's good," she says, still smiling. "We can reminisce later but right now we need to move; we don't have much time." She turns to go, but I don't move. She stops and looks at me questioningly, arms wide in exasperation.

"Jess, you know what I did, right? You know the risk you're taking if you help me?"

She walks back to me, puts her hands on my shoulders and fixes me with an intense stare. I notice green flecks in her now-smiling, hazel-colored eyes.

"Yes, I do, Frankie. And you are not responsible for my actions. Now, make like we're a couple and let's move." She takes my hand and sets off again. I fall in-step beside her, then, out of the corner of her mouth she adds, "I hated that bastard and I'm glad he's gone, glad you killed him." She turns and smiles at me cheekily. "And anyway, you're going to give me the exclusive story!"

I laugh out loud, admiring her spirit and relaxing a little. Regardless of our childhood connection, there's something about Jess that I instinctively trust, and right now I need all the help I can get.

We weave our way in silence through the city for the next fifteen minutes before entering a tree-lined street of once-grand homes, high up on the hillside rising to the west of the lake. Built with the crystal-flecked, purple granite native to the area, the houses are attractive and imposing. I assume they once belonged to the town's factory managers, now divided into neat apartments for striving professionals, like Jess; easily accessible from the hub of town but far enough away to provide a haven of peace and quiet. She lives in a turn of the century townhouse set in the middle of a row facing the lake.

We don't pass any other occupants as we enter the building and head up to her third-floor apartment. Her place is tastefully decorated in pastel colors, with a living room/kitchen combination at its center and a picture window framing the lake in the distance. There's a bathroom in one corner of the living room, and a bedroom next to it, also with a lake view. A second bedroom sits at the end of a hallway at right angles to the main living space, separate from the rest of the apartment.

Jess throws a towel at me and nods towards the bathroom. "The tramp look's no use anymore… and anyway, you smell bad," she says in a playful tone. "You need to clean up if you're going to be here. I'll get some coffee on."

I appreciate her directness, laugh in recognition of the truth of her words and head to the bathroom as instructed.

"Leave your clothes on the floor, I'll dump them later. I've got stuff here that'll fit you," she shouts after me.

It hadn't occurred to me that she might have a partner. The thought alarms me; involving a second person magnifies the risk.

As if reading my thoughts, Jess continues, "Don't worry, he moved out two months ago, left a few things he didn't want any more. Expected me to tidy up after him right until the end! He left a disposable razor too, in the cupboard – it's yours if you want it."

The shower's invigorating, and even though the razor's a little blunt, I manage a clean shave. There's a purple bruise on my jaw that's spreading down my neck, but it looks worse than it feels. It's good to be clean and tidy again.

I tie the towel around my waist and head into the living room, clutching my rucksack in front of me. A steaming mug of coffee is waiting, and draped across the back of Jess's worn, brown leather sofa are underwear, blue jeans and a red-and-black plaid shirt. She is leaning against the black granite kitchen counter, sipping her coffee and intently watching the TV news.

As I look around for somewhere to put my rucksack while I dress, Jess pipes up, "What is it with you and that thing?" I must look like a deer in headlights because she quickly continues, her eyes widening, "You've got something big in there, right?"

Awkwardly, I place the bag at my feet and try to avoid the question, but she pushes for an answer.

I have to say something. "Look, I have a document, Jess. It's an official government document that I'm not supposed to have. Can we leave it at that for now, please?"

She looks at me over the top of her coffee cup, evaluating whether to keep pushing. Her eyes are wide and excited, but I'm grateful that she decides discretion is the best path to take, at least for now.

"Sure. You'll tell me eventually anyway," she adds with a grin. "After all, I am an intrepid reporter, and you are the story of the moment, so my money is on that document being vital evidence."

I can feel my face redden, but I say nothing. Using the sofa as cover, I discreetly slip on the briefs and trousers. They're a good fit. But as I'm pulling on the shirt, Jess suddenly moves towards me, staring hard and pointing at my left side.

"Wow! What the heck did that to you?" she says, pointing at a livid red scar on my side.

Thicker at the back than at the front, it starts close to my kidneys and ends close to my liver, but neither organ was damaged. I quickly do up the shirt and tuck it in neatly.

"It's nothing, looks worse than it is. Just a souvenir from my first mission, a parting gift from a security guy working for my target." It's the simple truth, but the throwaway words sound shocking spoken aloud – by the size and location of the wound, it's clear that I could easily have been killed.

If Jess is shocked by my casual description, she doesn't show it. She just nods and lowers herself slowly into the high-backed, brown leather armchair set at an angle to the sofa, and nods for me to sit. I settle into the sofa and enjoy the soft give of well-worn leather.

"What happened?" she asks gently but with an edge that demands an answer.

I've never discussed my missions with anyone other than my commanders; I signed the Official Secrets Act. But everything changed three days ago when One Hundred and Thirteen died. And I owe Jess for helping me, for taking the risk.

I take a deep draft of the coffee. It's smooth and strong and kicks me into gear. "Almost all of my jobs were in the Middle East. In the last eight years, I've spent more time there than at home." I point to my side. "I got this gift on my first assignment though. Everything was so different and, at first, I hated it, being in the desert – freezing cold at night but instant, broiling heat once the sun rose. And the smells – earthy yet somehow fragrant. Not unpleasant, but just so different. Everything was different, and I was way out of my comfort zone. I just want to get the job done and get home. So, on that first job, I focused hard.

"'The job' was a drug lord called Yaron Chaban. Back then, I didn't ask what they'd done – if we needed them gone that was good enough for me. I knew from Chaban's background file that he would not be an easy hit, so I knew it could be a long wait. When my chance came, I'd been in position for almost thirty-eight hours, among the dunes half a mile above Chaban's compound. It was very secure: no clear shots available from any direction; no set pattern to Chaban's movements, except that he always left the compound once a day – but he always varied the time and was always in the comfort of his bullet-proof limo, which he kept in an underground garage accessed from inside the house, not to mention his four-man motorcycle guard, ready to defend against close-quarter attacks and respond quickly if threats came from further afield."

Jess nods and leans forward. "Frankie, would it be okay if I record this?"

The idea of going on the record is anathema to any serving wet-work operative. But things are different now. I nod my assent. Jess puts her cell phone on the coffee table between us, checks that it's recording and nods for me to continue.

"Everyone has a weakness though, no matter how careful and well prepared they are. From the background file I received before I left for the Middle East, I knew that Chaban had a vile temper that flared up unpredictably. Hot-heads make a mockery of even the best laid plans, so I knew he'd slip up if I was vigilant. And he did. Just once. But once was enough."

"You say you didn't ask what he'd done, but you must have wondered why our government thought he deserved to die?"

I take a long moment before I answer. "I know it seems absurd, but back then I really didn't. Honestly. That came later. All I knew then was that we wanted him dead, and it was my duty to make that happen." I shake my head at the memory. "Blind loyalty. Some would call it brainwashing, but everything I heard back then was a clear and consistent message, whether it came from my parents, my school, my church, my political party: we are righteous, we stand for freedom, we are a force for good in the world. I believed it all. At least, back then."

Jess nods and makes a note on the writing pad she's fished from her shoulder bag.

I take another sip of coffee, then continue, "That day, it was approaching ninety-five degrees when Chaban left the compound, just after 10am. I wore a headband to absorb the sweat from my forehead, to stop it getting into my eyes, but it was soon soaked, and sweat dripped off the end of my nose. Chaban's car rolled out of the compound unusually slowly, and that's when I noticed his hand extend out of the rear passenger window, fingers snapping in irritation. I was stunned – for security reasons, the only window that opens on our President's car is the driver's, and I had assumed Chaban's would be the same. Then his face appeared, contorted with rage. I saw a servant running to catch up, a Coca Cola can in his hand – Chaban loved his Coca Cola! He had a drinks' fridge in the car full of the stuff! It was usually restocked when he returned to the compound, but I guess that day his servants had messed up.

"Anyway, as Chaban leaned forward to take the can, still shouting, his head came into full view. I fixed him in my sight, took a deep breath, allowed for the distance, wind and heat, pulled the trigger, then breathed out. Chaban had a fifteen second lapse in discipline, but it was enough time for a single, clean, silenced shot."

"What did it feel like, to take another man's life like that?" Jess asked in a neutral tone.

I pause for a moment before answering, aware of the way I would come across. "At the time, it was just relief. Relief at a job well done and relief that I would soon be out of the desert. Other emotions crowded in later. His wife had died young and he had two sons under ten. If that had happened to my dad when I was that age, I would have been crushed, probably never have recovered. That thought haunts me now, but, at the time, I was running on adrenalin, focused on getting away. Our President wanted him gone so that was good enough for me."

Jess nods thoughtfully, and over her shoulder, on her sideboard, I notice a photo of a young boy with a beaming smile.

Jess follows my eyeline. "That's Alex, my son, on his birthday last year. He's fourteen now. He stays at his grandma's during the week – it's calmer, better for him to study." I pick up a pang of regret and want to understand more, but Jess quickly blocks the path, "I'm sorry," she says, "I interrupted your flow. So, what happened next?"

I make a mental note to ask about Alex another time. "The motorbike guards quickly got a broad fix on my position – it was the only area of the dunes the shot could have come from – and they set off immediately, engines screaming as they climbed the sand banks.

"I collected the spent shell casing and slipped down the dune to gather my gear. I could leave no trace. As I'd done each morning since I arrived, I'd already swept the area of all evidence of my visit and packed securely, ready to leave at a moment's notice. I carefully stowed my M110 and strapped the twenty-two-pound pack across my back. Then, I ran hard.

"I knew that satellite images of me on the move would have reached our base across the border in Sisipha and that a helicopter would already be in the air on its way to collect me. It was my responsibility to be at the collection point when it arrived. It would take me three minutes at a full sprint to reach the agreed location. As I ran, I calculated the time it would take the bikes to reach the top of the dune, scan the horizon, spot me and get within firing range. I assumed they'd know this desert well and use that knowledge to gain time. I knew it would be a close-run thing, so I ran harder than I'd ever run before.

"A change in engine sound told me Chaban's guards were already racing down the banks onto the plain – they'd closed the gap faster than I expected. I pushed harder, my legs and lungs burning, thick sand sucking me down, each stride more draining than the last. I heard the unmarked helicopter before I saw it, and accelerated to where I calculated it would come into view. Gasping now, the searing heat biting my throat, I reached the chopper as it rose above the dunes, hovering above the surface.

"Chaban's men opened fire, but their rounds dropped short. Two sets of hands reached out of the chopper, grabbed and hauled me aboard. Chaban's men closed in, and bullets fizzed and pinged off the fuselage as we banked away and climbed.

"Drenched in sweat, head bent between my knees and unable to speak, I sucked in air until my breathing and heartrate slowed. I straightened up and, still unable to speak, nodded thanks to the crew who'd hauled me aboard. One of them, a ruddy complexioned, stocky guy in his mid-thirties, with wrestler's ears and arms like tree boughs, said 'Looks like you need to learn how to run faster, son' and pointed at a crimson-stained slit in the right side of my tunic.

"Funny, the pain came only after I saw the blood, but then it came sharp and fierce. I ripped my shirt apart to get a better look – a vivid cut, half an inch wide, ran from the back to the front of my side. Just a flesh wound, but it hurt like hell."

To lighten the mood a little, I added, "Full-kit sprints have been part of my preparations ever since."

Jess didn't laugh, just topped up my coffee while she mulled something over. Then she said, "How many people have you killed for our government, Frankie?"

I don't hesitate. "One hundred twelve."

"And you never knew why you killed them, right?"

"That's right, at least not until number one hundred twelve. And that changed everything."

Jess's brow furrows, and I can tell that she wants to dig into that comment, explore the questions begging to be asked. I feel comfortable with her, but I don't know if I'm ready to answer all of her questions just yet. Her mouth opens to speak and then closes again, her attention drawn to the TV.

An image of me fills the screen, presumably captured by CCTV in the square – I couldn't have looked more like a tramp if I'd tried. Even though the sound is turned down low, the young male newsreader's excited body language conveys just how much trouble I'm in.

Jess turns up the volume as the young man enthuses: "A manhunt is underway in Basin Lake for Frankie Green, following a sighting by two local boys yesterday evening. Green is armed and dangerous, and members of the public are advised *not* to approach him. If you see him, call the number on the screen. I repeat, do not attempt to engage."

A national 800 number shows as Jess gives me a quizzical look. "Armed?" she says.

"I'm not," I reply, evenly. "They're saying it to keep people away – they want me for themselves, want to shut me up before anyone can hear what I have to say. There's good news though… they obviously don't know about you."

Jess nods thoughtfully. "True," she says.

CHAPTER TWELVE

The sound of heavy machinery catches our attention. Jess peers out the window overlooking the street.

"It's a troop carrier, ten men jumping out," she says. "They're pairing up, knocking on doors."

I grunt in recognition and ask, "What weapons can you see?"

"I'm no expert, but they look like short machine guns."

"They'll be C8 CQBs. Black Ops. They're spooked. Doing this in full view is not their MO. They're getting desperate, and they won't be asking questions if they find me."

A heavy thump below and muffled voices tells us they're in Jess's building. I grab my rucksack as Jess grabs my hand and pulls me along the hallway to the bedroom at the back of the apartment.

"In here," she says, and seeing my questioning look, adds, "No time to explain, just do it. Trust me."

I hear the door lock behind her as she runs back down the hallway to the apartment's main area. I stand with my back to the wall next to the door, ready to fight if it opens.

After a few minutes, I hear the Black Ops guys hammering on the front door.

"What the hell do you want?" Jess yells as she lets them in.

They don't respond. I hear them opening and closing cupboards in the lounge, then in the bedroom at the front of the apartment before heading down the hallway towards my hiding place. The door handle turns, then, finding it locked, the solider slams his shoulder into it. The frame gives a little but remains firm.

"Stop that, you idiot!" Jess screams.

"Unlock the door," a gruff voice demands.

"I don't have a key. And I don't have a key because that's not my apartment," Jess says, exasperation in her voice. "This was one big house when it was built, and this hallway ran all the way along the spine. They put the door in when the place was divided into apartments. I guess anyone wealthy enough could rent the whole top floor and leave that door open, but that ain't me, so it's locked. And neither I nor Mrs. Sullivan next door have a key!"

She sounds convincing. If I didn't know the truth I'd probably believe her. The Black Ops team evidently does. They grunt their apologies and leave the apartment at the double to continue the search.

I sit on the bed, let out a long, slow breath and hang my head between my knees. I hear the lock mechanism click, then Jess pokes her head in.

"All clear," she says.

I follow her into the living room, seriously impressed by her coolness.

She says over her shoulder, "I know what you're thinking, but just keep in mind that I'm a journalist – most of us love the truth, it's just that getting to the truth sometimes requires you to lie like a pro!"

We both laugh, but I'm conscious that it's just a matter of time before the truth is discovered. I don't need to explain, Jess has clearly already reached the same conclusion; she slips into her bedroom and emerges with a small, battered, brown suitcase and a long, red coat.

Reading my raised eyebrows, she lifts the case and says, "You never know when a story might require a trip, so I always keep one packed, ready to go."

I grab my discarded desert gear and follow her out of the apartment and along the hallway to the fire escape at the back of the building, listening out for the Black Ops team as we go. Once outside the building, we trot down the black, metal steps to the ground, maneuver through an area of waste containers and emerge at the back of the houses onto a quiet, narrow lane that runs parallel to Jess's Street. Weeds push through the asphalt and it's strewn with junk.

She takes my hand and turns right. We walk steadily so as not to draw attention and emerge about a quarter of the way down a street that runs perpendicular to Jess's. It's lined with the same style of grand house and runs downhill to the lake.

I glance left and see the search party gathering at the top of Jess's Street. We quicken our pace. Jess points a key fob at a black Toyota Land Cruiser parked diagonally across the street; she jumps behind the wheel while I stow her case and my rucksack in the back seat. I then watch in silence as she flips open the back of her cell phone, takes out the SIM card and carefully inserts it in a slit in her phone's cover, then slips the phone into the glove compartment and removes another phone, still in its plastic wrapping, and in just a few seconds sets it up for use.

"Force of habit," she says. "We often track people using their phone signals, so whenever I want to be off the grid, I disable mine and set up a cheap burner. Oh, and in case you're worried, the car's not in my name – my ex registered it." She winks at me, clearly enjoying herself. "As far as the Department of Motor Vehicles knows, I don't even own a car."

I carefully watch the search party in the rear-view mirror as we pull out then, seeing no signs of interest in us, I relax in my black leather seat and look around. The car is clean and smells faintly of a perfume I recognize but can't name. Jess smoothly navigates her way to the 201 and heads east, away from the city.

Processing Jess's calm, I wonder who exactly I'm caught up with. I remember the spunky kid from summer school way back when, I remember that I loved to spend time with her, but other than that, I don't know much about her at all. I have no idea where she's taking me but, for some reason, that doesn't worry me. I wonder why.

CHAPTER THIRTEEN

As we pass the city limits, Jess hands me her burner phone and asks me to dial a number she knows by heart.

While I'm tapping at the black keys on the phone's cream-colored keyboard, she explains, "I just need to speak to Sylvie real quick – she's the camerawoman with me when we met you in Oakvale." My face must convey my concern because she quickly continues, "It's okay, I won't mention you."

Sylvie picks up immediately, and I hand the phone back to Jess.

"Hey, Sylv, can't say too much right now, but something's come up and it's big, so please clear my decks for the next few days and make my apologies to anyone I'm meant to be meeting. I'll be in touch again real soon, okay?" I hear Sylvie's muffled agreement, then Jess wraps up the call, saying, "And make a note of this number – yep, the usual routine's in play. This is my burner for now. Okay, gotta run. Talk soon."

Jess slips the phone into her door's side pocket, and we lapse into silence, lost in our own thoughts as the highway stretches out before us.

As the city gives way to the countryside and the traffic thins, we follow the four-lane road through a steep valley, gouged out of the volcanic rock at the height of the last ice age. Its layers of ash laid down over centuries and crushed into layers of rock each bear a different color. In each layer, quartz crystals shimmer in the afternoon light – they're a welcome distraction, and I try to enjoy their patterns, but my thoughts keep coming back to the present.

Jess focuses intently on the road ahead, the same determination on her face as I remember seeing when we first met all those years ago – it makes me smile, and I count myself lucky to have met her again. But I know it can't continue.

I break the silence. "Jess, I can't thank you enough for what you've done. Really. But you know I can't let you take any more risks on my behalf, right? Please just let me out wherever works for you, and I'll take it from there."

Jess grips the steering wheel tight and laughs loud and hard, her eyes bright, the determination in her face replaced by a stunning smile. "You have to be kidding, right? This is the biggest story this country has ever seen, and right now, I have an exclusive. There's no way I'm letting you out of my sight, Frankie Green."

I can't help laughing at her brutal logic, but I persist, my voice rising slightly, "Look, they've already tried to kill me, and they will keep trying. I can't put you in harm's way, it's just wrong. And what about Alex? If you get hurt when they try again, what then?"

Her expression darkens and she's quiet for a while.

When she next speaks, her voice is soft and tinged with sadness. "Truth is, I haven't been a great mom to Alex. Too much time chasing two-bit headlines, not enough time listening to his own stories, his day-to-day experiences, his highs and lows." She pauses and then adds, never taking her eyes off the road, "And he lives with my mom full-time, not just at weekends. And it's out of choice, not necessity. His choice."

She's quiet again, staring at the road, her jaw working hard as she fights back tears.

"I guess I just want him to be proud of me, you know? And what you did – well, that story just must be told. It's huge. And sooner rather than later. After all, our country claims to be the beacon of free speech in the world – if you get hurt once the story's out and before trial, the entire world's press will point the finger straight at us, and that's something the government would hate even more than whatever you have to say."

I'm touched by Jess's honesty and impressed by her clarity, though I still have doubts. "I'm not sure anything would embarrass our government these days… but I see your logic, it's good. But I will not see you hurt, so I have one ground rule: if it comes to violence, I do the fighting, okay?"

Jess laughs and, still smiling, says, "I've got a rule of my own, Frankie Green: I do the planning. I know how this country works way better than you do; while you were out in the desert, I was following the grubby paths carved by the great and good of this land. They will eat you alive if you try to go it alone."

I think back over the last few days and recognize the truth in what she's said. I nod my agreement.

She glances across at me – more an evaluative stare – then appears to reach a decision. "So, I have an idea… maybe a bit whacky… but, how about we set up a broadcast – me interviewing you – and then flood social media? It'll get picked up by every network in the world and every internet app, too. It'll get the word out loud and clear so that, if they do manage to bring you into custody, the world will already know what happened, right? That's got to give you some cover, get you your day in court!"

The idea sounds so absurd that I laugh out loud. "So, we just borrow a studio and start broadcasting?"

"Not quite, but I know a place we can make it happen." Jess says it so confidently that it makes me sit up in my seat. "We'll broadcast live across all the major social platforms. The government will scramble to shut it down, but it'll be like a genie – once it's out of the bottle there's no way to put it back, especially when the networks get their hands on it."

For the first time in days, I feel a flutter of hope.

CHAPTER FOURTEEN

Jess fishes out her burner phone and hits redial. Sylvie picks up after three rings, and Jess launches in before Sylvie can say a word. "Sylv. The huge story I mentioned, well, it's on. I have the man of the moment with me now!" I can hear a flurry of excitement but I can't make out exactly what Sylvie's asking. Jess cuts her short. "Listen, I need you to meet me at Starvation Peak Studio as soon as you can – I'm on my way now, should be there in a couple of hours. And please stop by my mom's, let her and Alex know I can't make this weekend. Oh, and while you're there, could you pick up my 'TV clothes' – Mom will know what that means. If you leave now you won't be too far behind. See you soon!"

I faintly hear Sylvie's excited agreement, then Jess hangs up and glances my way. Seeing my questioning look, she explains, "Starvation Peak's up in the mountains, kinda spartan and isolated but surrounded by beauty. It was huge in the 70s – lots of Rock bands' 'concept albums' were inspired by the mountain air, the tree-covered valleys and the ridgelines that stretch for miles around. Pete Palmer ran the place until he died a couple of years back, and it's been closed since; Pete had a 'complicated' personal life, and his estate's been locked up in legal battles between his ex-wives and his brothers. Warring relatives – you know how it goes when people get a sniff of money."

Actually, I don't – we never had any, and no one in Oakvale did either, but I nod anyway.

"The good news for us," she continues, "is the studio's got great equipment and it's pretty much as it was on his last day… and guess what? I know the door key code!" Jess adds triumphantly. I'm about to ask her how come she knows the code, but she anticipates the question. "You don't want to know. Let's just say Pete's younger brother and I had a thing for a while."

Her beaming smile is infectious, and I smile at her excitement as I relax into my seat. Jess has the bit between her teeth, just like I remember her when we played soccer at summer camp. She focuses intently on the road ahead, while I try to organize my thoughts about what I'll say when we reach the studio.

But I can't focus. My mind wanders back to what Jess shared about her mom looking after Alex.

"How often do you get to see Alex, Jess?"

She answers stiffly and grips the steering wheel more tightly. She doesn't turn her head and keeps her focus firmly on the road. "Every weekend." She sighs. "I drive up after work on Friday and head back to the city on Sunday evening."

"I can't imagine how tough that is, Jess – I don't have children, never married, but I know that would eat away at me."

She swallows hard and nods but forces a brighter tone as she replies, "But, you know, it's great for Alex. Mom lives on a five-acre plot, mainly woodland and ponds. She has neighbors, but they're ten minutes away by car, so when Alex is done studying, he just plays outdoors, climbs trees, sets up camp, that sort of thing. That's got to be way better for him than being pent up in a city apartment playing video games, right? And, of course, Mom loves having him there – Dad died when I was twelve, and she never remarried, so Alex is great company for her – they're really close."

I nod. "I get it. I would certainly have loved that as a kid. I'm just sorry it doesn't work better for you."

Jess silently reaches across and squeezes my hand. We both lose ourselves in thought as the miles click by.

CHAPTER FIFTEEN

After a while, I break the silence. "I voted for him, you know. Both times."

Jess glances across at me, eyebrows raised in surprise.

She says nothing, so I continue, "The first time, I was completely bought in, like everyone else in Oakvale. When he came to our town – held one of his rallies there – it was electric. The cheering and chanting before he came on, it was like nothing I'd felt before; the noise made my whole body vibrate. The town had been so quiet, depressed even, and then he came and everyone's spirits lifted – suddenly I'm surrounded by bright, shiny faces with eyes alive with hope. It was exhilarating."

Jess is trying hard to find a neutral expression, but I can read the incredulity in her eyes.

I chuckle softly. "Yeah, I know. I really do know – you don't need to say it. Looking back at it now, it sounds incredible to me, too. But, back then, it seemed like he understood our pain – spoke our language. Massively rich but as though he really 'got us' little guys, and he really did seem to care. He knew what we needed and he seemed so confident, so in our corner, like no politician we'd ever seen. When he said he'd bring back the jobs, we believed him, absolutely. When he told us his opponent was a no-hope loser, we cheered him so loud, and when he swore the negative press was all part of a plot to stop him getting us out from under the boot of 'the man', we couldn't wait for him to get started. We were ready to go to war for him! All of us. No exceptions."

We sit in silence for a moment.

"There were signs even back then, though," I continue. "Signs of what he was really like. But we laughed them off – didn't want to give life to anything that could tarnish the hopes he'd lit of a return to a bright future for Oakvale.

"I wasn't as quick to jump on board as most folks were, and my parents were slow too, for the same reason. We were raised to value honesty – to never duck the truth, no matter how difficult that might sometimes be – so his lies really bothered us, and his court cases and the wriggling to avoid the consequences of his actions. That's just not right, never will be. But whenever I discussed it with friends, they'd shut me down fast, saying things like 'Sure, I could do without the rhetoric too, but Frankie, the man's a winner and he'll win for us' or, sometimes more bluntly, 'Get over it and get on board. We need him.' So, I swallowed hard and got on board.

"I met him for the first time not long after his first inauguration; in fact, he pinned my first medal on me, for the Chaban killing. It was at a ceremony in the Great House for a small group of service members like me. Our families were there, too. We were all so proud and so star-struck to be in the presence of the man everyone saw as their savior. But there were the warning signs then, too: he asked each of us a bunch of questions but he didn't listen to the answers; and his eyes were cold, no warmth at all. At least not until he shook Mom's hand after the ceremony, and she gushed about how grateful she was that he was saving our country, making us great again. He loved that, couldn't get enough of it!"

"So, what happened?" Jess asks. "Why the change of heart?"

Before I can answer, her phone rings.

CHAPTER SIXTEEN

"Hey Sylv, you on the road yet?" Jess says, then she slams on the brakes and brings the car to a halt on the roadside. A truck swerves past us as she puts the phone on speaker.

The next voice is male. With chillingly calm intonation that I know but can't immediately place, he says to Jess, "Tell us where he is, and we'll let your mom and son go."

Jess's face drains to white, her eyes widen in fear and tears spill down her cheeks. She looks at me pleadingly, her mouth open but unable to speak.

I take the decision out of her hands. "I'll come in," I say, loud and clear.

"Smart boy, Frankie," he responds. He has a slight lisp, and this time I match the voice to a name – Daniel Molinar, another one I trained with. He's short for a soldier but very powerfully built. And he's good. Utterly ruthless.

"Stay put, Frankie, we've triangulated your signal now. We've got the coordinates. We'll come to you."

I know this tactic: ultimate deniability. He knows we're in the middle of nowhere, sitting ducks. If I agree, we'll end up buried in a ditch. "Not a chance, Danny. We'll come to you."

Molinar thinks for a moment. It's a good offer. They're already in situ and can prepare for our arrival. The odds would be all in their favor.

"Okay, Frankie, as you like. But no messing – come straight here. We'll be tracking you." He hangs up.

Jess stares at me desperately, rocking backwards and forwards in her seat. "How? How did they know? Did I screw up?" Her voice rises to a shout. "Have I put my son and mother in danger?"

I reach across, pull her close and hug her. "No, you didn't screw up, Jess," I say quietly. "They just got lucky. They would have figured out you'd lied back at the apartment, then you disappeared; two unusual events, not necessarily incriminating or even connected, but they had to consider the possibility that you were with me and check it out. They'd have looked first at your family and friends, and your mom's is the obvious place to start. That would have been fine – none of your family knows a thing about me – so, they'd have dropped the lead quickly once they'd established that, but then I imagine Sylvie showed up! Not her fault either, just bad timing."

Jess nods her understanding. She's quiet for a moment and slowly her sobs stop.

She thumps the steering wheel and spits, "If they harm one hair on Alex's head, or my mom's, I swear I'll tear them limb from limb." She looks across at me, her face angry and determined. "Let's get the fuckers out of my mom's home."

CHAPTER SEVENTEEN

I know Molinar wouldn't think twice about killing Alex or Jess's mom, but I admire Jess's fight, and I know she'll need it.

"Let's make sure they don't get a chance to hurt them, Jess. Tell me about your mom's place. Have a think about the lay of the land, anything I could potentially use."

She focuses immediately on the task at hand. Her body remains tense, but solving tangible problems seems to calm her, give her focus. While she's thinking, I take the chance to remove from my rucksack the file I took when One Hundred and Thirteen died and stash it in the glove compartment amongst the vehicle registration and insurance papers. Not much of a hiding place, but they'll scour each place we stop along the way, so it's as good as any.

Finally, Jess says, "It's pretty much farmland round there. There's a small community called Lilly Springs about ten minutes away, with a school and maybe twenty houses, but from there to Mom's, farms are spread out in every direction with acres of land between them." Then a thought lands heavily, creasing her brow. "I guess they could hit us anywhere along that road, right? But it's the only way in!"

It's a natural concern but not a real risk. "Too public," I say. "Any one of those farms could see the hit and report it. They'll want to do this quietly."

"What does that mean, Frankie? I mean concretely, specifical-ly – do what?"

I pause for a moment. I want to be open but I don't want to scare her; when the time comes, she'll need to focus.

Then her feisty spirit rears up again as another thought strikes her: "Frankie, you can't go quietly! You can't do that!" she shouts, her eyes wide.

I'm touched by how much she cares but am not really sure why. I look into her wide, pretty, hazel eyes, and the same frisson of connection I felt when we first reunited back in Oakvale re-turns – and it's just as electric. I fight to ignore it, but the look in her eyes tells me she feels it, too.

I let go of her hands and look down, trying to focus on our next step. I shift in my seat and keep looking forward until the moment passes.

"I have no intention of going quietly, Jess. Not at all. But I will do absolutely nothing to endanger any of you. You have my word on that."

She stares at me intently, her body taut. Finally, she lets out a long, slow breath as the tension leaves her. Then she says, "Okay, so, how do we get everyone out?"

It's a fair question, but I'm scrambling again outside my area of expertise. "Honestly, I don't exactly know yet. But when we're there, and I see the lay of the land, I will know exactly what to do. Trust me."

We drive on in silence, and I hope my confidence is not mis-placed!

CHAPTER EIGHTEEN

We make good time and reach Lilly Springs just as its white clapboard homes and well-tended gardens take on a golden hue in the setting sun. It's a peaceful, charming place, oozing slowness and calm. The road out of town follows the contours of the land over gentle hills dotted with cows chewing happily on a carpet of lush grass. We press on, increasingly tense and anxious, keeping at a steady speed; we're aware of the drone shadowing us but are focused on what lies ahead.

After a few miles, Jess turns into her mom's sweeping, graveled driveway, which slopes gently down the hillside through ranch-style gates then widens into a parking area in front of an imposing, brick-built house. Two steps flanked by stone-carved lions lead up to a heavy looking, red-painted wooden door. A gleaming brass door knocker sits at its center. Symmetrically set either side of the door are leaded windows, with a matching pair above them on the second story.

As we come to a stop, Molinar steps out from the shadows of a vine-covered pergola to the right of the house, the gravel crunching under his feet, a silenced revolver in his right hand. He's dressed in a dark suit, white shirt and tie – not conventional operational gear, but there will have been a reason for the choice. There always is.

I glance at Jess, expecting to see fear in her eyes. Instead, I see simmering anger.

I reach across and take her tightly balled fists into my hands. "Breathe, Jess. Just try to stay calm, it's going to be okay. Alex and your mom will be just fine. Trust me."

She grunts acceptance but her molten gaze never leaves Molinar, who's stepped forward and swung open the passenger side door for me to get out.

"Well, well, if it isn't Frankie Green?! Top of the class in training camp now gone rogue." He stops speaking, waiting for a reaction.

I don't give him one but swing out of the truck and stand facing him. I'm almost a foot taller, but he has the build of an ox and the kind of face that only a mother could love – a nose like a sharpened axe jutting out of an otherwise flat face and narrow, pale blue eyes that are icy cold.

Jess gets out of the car and comes to stand beside me. I'm about to speak, but she beats me to it, "Where are my mom and son, you asshole? You better not have hurt them or so help me God, I'll tear your fucking head off!"

I look sideways at Jess, partly in admiration, partly in dread that she'll push Molinar too far.

Unperturbed, he smiles cruelly at me. "Wow, Frankie, you've certainly got a feisty one there!" Then, turning his attention to Jess, he says, "They're safe, my dear." And then adds after a short pause, "At least for now."

Jess starts towards him, gravel spitting out from under her feet and clattering against the side of the truck – I need to use all my strength to pull her back.

Hugging her close, her breathing ragged and her face red with anger, I whisper into her ear and stare hard at Molinar, "It's okay. It's all going to be fine, Jess."

She hugs me tight and her shoulders shake as the tears start.

"Happy now, Molinar? Good to see that some things never change – you're still a Grade A shit."

Molinar nods in satisfaction and moves towards us with two sets of plastic restraining cuffs, saying, "Well, enough of the pleasantries, let's get on with this shall we?"

"Hold your hands out in front," I whisper quickly to Jess, and I do the same, hoping that Molinar is enjoying the moment so much that he won't force us to put our hands behind our backs. I breathe a sigh of relief when he takes the bait.

The steps up to the house lead into a wood-paneled hallway lit by a crystal chandelier; highly polished, black-and-white floor tiles reflect its light brightly. There's a pervasive smell of fresh flowers mixed with furniture polish.

Molinar follows close behind as we walk along the hallway towards the back of the house. To my right we pass an elegant dining room, with a huge oak table surrounded by finely carved chairs, and to the left, a plushly furnished, red-carpeted living room.

"Nice place your mom's got, Jess – you didn't tell me she was loaded," I say, hoping to lighten her mood.

Jess smiles briefly but continues to look straight ahead.

We pass another open door on the right, with narrow steps leading down, presumably to a cellar.

"Next room on the right," Molinar barks.

I glance ahead and see the open door he wants us to enter and then notice another heavy oak door opposite, this one closed.

Jess follows my gaze and says, "That's the kitchen."

I nod, and together we enter the room Molinar wants us in. It's a large space flooded with light courtesy of a huge picture window. The sun's rays reflect off soft yellow, patterned wallpaper, and a huge TV sits above a stone-carved fireplace. It would normally be a delightful room, but now it reeks of sweat and fear, discordantly out of place amongst the expensive-looking sofas and classy coffee tables.

Through the window, a rose garden in full bloom stands in stark contrast to the two huge, grim-faced, armed guards standing in front of the French doors that lead out to it. Both men remain silent and barely acknowledge our arrival. One is several years younger than the other, presumably the older man's trainee; both have buzz cuts, and, like Molinar, they are dressed in suits and ties, which sit awkwardly on their over-muscled frames.

Jess's mom and Alex are seated side by side on fine oak dining chairs, with their hands bound by plastic ties behind the chair backs. Jess's mom is pretty, with her gray hair cut into a bob. She's smartly dressed in slacks and a light pink sweater – she looks trim and healthy. Jess looks a lot like her. Alex is sitting next to his grandma, in jeans and a black T-shirt. The family resemblance is remarkable – he's the spitting image of Jess. He also looks physically okay. But, while they're not in physical pain, they are clearly both distressed; tear tracks stain their cheeks. My heart goes out to them; the trauma they've already endured will haunt them for years. And it's not over yet, not by a long way.

Jess runs over and tries awkwardly to hug them despite her cuffs. The guards glance down, see no danger, and focus on me instead. I don't know either of them, but I recognize that look – they can't wait for the action to start.

"Where's Sylvie?" I say.

"Oh, she's a little under the weather, Frankie," Molinar says. "Took a bit of persuading to call young Jess here."

Alex screams at Molinar, "You're a fucking animal! He beat her black and blue. She's on the floor in the kitchen. She was out cold when they dragged us in here."

"Like mother, like son, eh, Frankie?" Molinar says icily, taking a step towards Alex, his hand raised to strike him.

In an instant, Jess puts herself between them, but Molinar swats her away, and she crumples onto the finely carved stone hearth beneath the TV.

I move to help her up. Simultaneous clicking sounds tell me that three locked and loaded guns are now pointing at my back.

Staying calm and, without looking at them, I say, "Calm down, Molinar, and call the dogs off." I hear three more clicks and know they've done as I asked.

I lift Jess out of the fireplace and help her to the sofa nearest her mom and Alex. She's shaken but unhurt – and still as angry as a wasps' nest.

I whisper into her ear, "Try to stay calm, Jess. We'll be out of here soon." Then, I turn to Molinar. "So, what's it to be, Danny? Shoot me here or go somewhere more discrete?"

"All in good time, Frankie. I have a few questions for you first. Shall we?" There's a cruel inflection in his words as he gestures for me to leave the room ahead of him.

I glance back and wink at Jess, and force a smile at Alex and Jess's mom. They smile back weakly. I need them to stay strong.

Molinar addresses the guards, "Just keep an eye on them for now, okay. I might need them to help loosen Frankie's tongue."

I curse inwardly. He's remembered my weak spot from training – every person has one, and mine is that I can't stand causing innocent people harm. He'll use that. I'll need to act fast so he doesn't get the chance. Happily, with my memory of training twigged, I remember Molinar's major weakness, too: his arrogance sometimes makes him sloppy.

I think about that as the guards acknowledge Molinar's instruction, then we leave the room with the barrel of his gun against the small of my back.

CHAPTER NINETEEN

I see my opportunity as soon as we start down the staircase. The steps are narrow and steep; Molinar is comfortable with this because he has a gun and I don't, but he doesn't seem to notice that each time I step down, the height advantage I have on a flat surface is reduced and my head becomes almost level with his. He should have anticipated this and stayed a step higher all the way down – heads can be powerful weapons. I have to be patient, though. I can't make my move until we're almost at the bottom. If it works, it'll rock his brain and cause his brain stem to twist, but I'm only guessing where his nose is, so I need a little luck.

I move steadily so he continues to feel like he's in control, but three steps from the bottom, I lean forward slightly, tighten my core and then whip my head backwards, fast and hard. When I hear a sharp crack, I know I've caught him exactly where I wanted to – on the bridge of his nose – and when I feel the pressure of his weight on my back, I know he's out cold.

I brace and unsteadily carry him on my back down the last few steps, lower him quietly onto the brick floor and collect his gun. I point it at his head; everything I learned in training tells me to pull the trigger, eliminate an enemy and even up the odds. But I can't. This is Jess's family home, and if I kill him here it will be ruined for them forever.

Molinar is lying face down, unconscious, blood streaming from his nose. The skin around his eyes is already turning black. He won't be unconscious for long, and by the time he wakes I need to have tied him up. But first, I must get myself free of the plastic ties around my wrists.

As I look around the room, I realize that what I thought was a cellar is actually a boiler room and, to my surprise, we're not underground – a door leads from the room to the back garden. When the house was built, the architect clearly took advantage of the farmland's rolling contours so that what looks like a regular two-story house at the front is actually three stories at the back.

I begin to scour the floor and then run my hands along the shelves that line the walls, looking for anything I can use to loosen the ties. Eventually, on the floor, beneath what looks like an old pipe repair, I find a sliver of metal, about an eighth of an inch wide and an inch long. I pinch it between the thumb and forefinger of my right hand and then twist my wrists until I can see the black plastic clasp that Molinar pushed down to tighten the cuffs. It's awkward, but I eventually get an angle and work the metal down between the solid plastic edge of the clasp and the cuff strap. A gap gradually opens up and, by the time I've forced the sliver of metal all the way through to the other side, it is wide enough for me to slide my hand out. With my left-hand free, I repeat the process on the other side, much faster this time.

Molinar's breathing heavily and moving sluggishly on the floor, trying to get his head clear enough to stand. I stride over and stamp on the back of his head, crunching his nose into the tile. He grunts loudly and is completely still.

After confirming that he's breathing, I drag him to the boiler feeder pipe, put his arms behind his back and loop my old plastic ties around the pipe and his wrists, tightening them fully. When he wakes up, he'll be going nowhere fast; every effort he makes to loosen the cuffs will only draw them tighter.

I want him to stay quiet when he comes round, so I slip off his tie and stuff it into his mouth. I then take one of his shoelaces and thread it through his mouth, over the tie and round his head to keep the tie in place. He'll work it out of his mouth eventually, but it'll give me a little extra time. And I might need it.

***

I need to check on Sylvie in the kitchen. Using the stairs is too risky, so I slip out of the boiler room door into the garden and scan the area for back-up guards prowling the grounds. I don't really expect to see any; the three of them should have been plenty for this mission – losing us all will put a major dent in Molinar's career plans. The thought makes me smile.

To my left, up a steep bank, is the rose garden, and beyond that is the kitchen. To my right is a brick wall that runs down the length of the garden to a hedge at the bottom. Climbing the bank brings the risk of being seen, but at least I'll be able to see what's happening to Jess and her family. And, once at the top, I should be able to skirt around the back to what I hope will be an unlocked kitchen door.

I quickly snake my way up the bank and duck behind the rear row of roses. The sweet, spicy smell gives a lift to my senses. I can see that the situation in the room is unchanged: the guards remain at their stations, watchful but unconcerned; Jess and her family are silent, staring hopefully at the door I left through. I scamper across the remainder of the rose garden on all fours and emerge into a second parking area at the rear of the house. I trot up the side of the house and open the first door I come to, assuming it must be the kitchen. I quietly step inside.

Brightly colored Spanish tiles cover the floor, high-end kitchen equipment lines the walls and an ornate island dominates the center of the room, surrounded by high-back wicker chairs. From a burnished iron strip above the island, heavy cast-iron pans hang. Beyond the island, in the far corner, facing the door, Sylvie is curled into a ball on the floor.

She sits up awkwardly as I approach. I can see that her hands are tied behind her back and her face is bruised and bloodied. Her swollen eyes stare at me imploringly – she's not sure if I mean her harm. She's not gagged, so I put my finger to my lips to signal her to stay quiet and then I cut her loose with the scissors from a varnished wooden knife block on the island.

She sobs as she puts two and two together and realizes who I am, then quickly regains her composure. I quietly explain the predicament Jess, her mom and Alex are in, and she can't stop grinning when I explain how we're going to free them.

CHAPTER TWENTY

Sylvie's scream is loud, piercing, insistent and unignorable, and it provokes the response we hoped for. The younger guard pushes open the kitchen door and strides in angrily, gun drawn, but when he sees me leaning against the cabinets where he expected to see Sylvie, he stops in his tracks and his mouth drops open. With the perfect timing that accompanies the delivery of karmic justice, Sylvie hits him squarely in the groin with the steel frying pan from the set above the island. I watch as the white-hot, knife-stabbing pain that follows buckles his knees, and the air is sucked from his body. He drops to the floor and curls up in a ball, hands clasped between his legs. I push the door closed behind him while Sylvie brings the pan down hard on the top of his head, stunning him. With twine we found in the pantry, we tie his hands and feet behind his back, stuff a dish towel into his mouth and lay him face down behind the island.

I collect his gun and phone, and head across the hallway.

The older guard bellows from within the other room, "Davey, what the fuck's going on in there? Get back here now."

He's halfway to the door as I enter the room with the young guard's gun cocked and ready. He reaches for his weapon but stops, recalling what I do for the army and realizing that he'd be dead before his gun was drawn.

Sylvie comes in behind me. I keep my gun trained on the guard as she cuts Jess, Alex and Jess's mom free. Out of the corner of my left eye I watch them shake their feet and hands to get the circulation going again.

Spotting a set of plastic restraints bulging from the big guy's jacket pocket, I point and say, "Sylvie, pass me those, please."

To my surprise, it's Alex who responds. Tall for his age and with the easy, rangy movement of an athlete, he confidently strides over and whips the ties from the man's pocket, then throws them perfectly for me to make an easy catch.

As I tie the guard, they all make their way into the rose garden for some fresh air and a renewed sense of freedom. I'm trained to deal with the kind of trauma they've endured, they aren't; I will need to keep a close eye on them.

Once tied up, I push the guard to the back of the plush red sofa facing the fireplace. He tries to get himself upright but sinks back each time. With a resigned sigh, he realizes that, with his hands tied, he's not able to leverage his bulky frame out of the steeply cambered seat; he'll be stuck there until help comes.

I take his weapon and his phone from his inside pocket. As I leave the room, I say, "Don't worry, I'll let HQ know where to find you."

He grimaces at the thought of their arrival. Black Ops take a dim view of failed missions.

CHAPTER TWENTY-ONE

I ask everyone to wait at the front of the house while I make one last check on each of our prisoners. Satisfied that they are no threat, I stuff black trash sacks that I found in the kitchen with bottles of water, soft drinks and food that requires no cooking from the cupboards. As I leave the house, I drop the SIM cards from the guards' phones into a vase in the hallway.

As I step out of the front door, I'm almost knocked off my feet; everyone clammers round, hugging and thanking me. I know this level of emotion, it's just a normal physical reaction when extreme stress ends – the euphoria of release. So, I let them have a moment and then gently free myself, take a step backwards and wait for them to quieten down. They feel safe now and remain calm as I lay out our next steps.

"Okay, okay, all we've won is a battle, not the war. And I'm sorry to tell you that now we need to stick together until this is over, all of us." I check the reactions of Alex and Jess's mom. They look surprised, so I address them directly, "You won't be safe here. Black Ops will clean up, and you cannot trust any form of authority - not the police, not the politicians and plainly not the military – until this is over. What you've just witnessed makes you targets, so we have to stick together now, okay?"

They still look thoughtful, but then Jess's mom puts her arm around Alex's shoulders and says, "Makes sense." Alex nods his understanding.

I'm about to continue when I feel a sudden urge to introduce myself to Jess's mom properly. "Look, I really am sorry you got dragged into this, and I wish we'd met in different circumstances, but please allow me to introduce myself. I'm Frankie, Captain Frankie Green." I hold out my hand.

She beams at me as she takes it and shakes it warmly. Glancing across at Jess, she says, "So nice to meet a young man with manners."

Jess rolls her eyes.

Then she says, "Yes, I could wish things were different, too, but it's still nice to meet you, Frankie Green. I'm Shirley, but you can call me Shirl."

"Okay, so, Shirl, I want you to know that your house will still be here and just as beautiful when all this is over, and those men in there will soon be gone. Please don't worry about that. But, in the meantime, Black Ops will have called for an update and, when they got no response, will have got on their way here. We need to get moving."

Sylvie chimes in, "We're still doing the interview, right?"

I nod, but before I can speak, Jess takes the bags of food and drink from me and says, "Okay, so my truck can fit us all in. Let's get going."

I'm about to raise an issue, but Alex beats me to it, "Hold on a second, Mom. If I've got this right, I don't think that's a good plan." He glances at me, and I nod for him to continue. "The truck and probably all the other vehicles here are compromised. They know all about them and they'll be watching for them, right Frankie?"

"That's right, Alex," I say, smiling at the prideful look he is unsuccessfully trying to hide. "So, our first challenge is to find transport."

Shirley interrupts my flow, "No problem, I have that one covered." She points behind the rose garden.

Jess lets out a raucous laugh. "You still got that old thing, Mom? I thought you sold it when Dad died."

"I planned to, Jess, but it holds too many memories – I just couldn't let it go. I still go sit in it from time to time, just soaking up the smells and reliving the memories of all those trips we made when you were young."

"Okay, that's great," I say. "Let's take a look in a moment, but first I need to check something with you, Sylvie."

Sylvie's face is bruised and she's moving awkwardly, obviously in some pain. They must have worked her over hard to force her to call Jess, and I can't help wondering what else she might have told them.

Sylvie looks at me open faced, ready to help. I feel bad for asking, but I must. "Sylvie, did you share any of our plans with them?"

Jess is instantly angry and yells at me, "Of course not! She'd never do that, would you Sylv?"

Sylvie looks thoughtful. "Honestly, I don't even know whether I would or not. They hurt me bad, Jess, and he's right to check. Truth is, though, they never asked. So, no, Frankie, no worries about heading to the studio. That's still the best option – they don't know about it."

Jess takes my hand, squeezes it gently and whispers, "Sorry for sounding off."

I squeeze back to indicate that all's fine.

We follow Shirley past the kitchen, through the rose garden and down a manicured lawn with a pretty duck pond towards a Dutch barn set off to the left of the property.

CHAPTER TWENTY-TWO

When Shirley draws back the barn doors, I'm amazed to see a slightly rusty but otherwise well cared for, two-tone VW Camper Van in the center of the floor. It has white upper and avocado green lower parts, and it'll seat us all comfortably, but it must have been made more than twenty-five years ago.

"Does it still go?" I ask.

"Let's find out, shall we," Shirley says confidently as she slips into the driver's seat.

With the choke drawn out fully, the engine revs on the first turn of the key and black smoke sputters from the exhaust.

Now certain that we can get moving, I instruct everyone to quickly grab a change of clothes from the house and anything else they'll need – unless it's in one of the rooms where the Black Ops guys are. I then run back to Jess's truck to retrieve my gear.

When I get to the truck, I'm relieved to find my rucksack is still there. I'm even more relieved when I check the glove compartment and remove the document I stashed there, Jess's second burner phone and the phone she dismantled when we set off from Basin Lake.

On the way back to the VW, I throw her first burner in the pond.

***

Sylvie slips into the passenger seat and chats comfortably with Shirley, who insists on driving. Jess and Alex take the second row; they're both asleep within minutes of us setting off, Jess's arm around her son's shoulders.

I take the back row and worry about what could go wrong. Black Ops will certainly put up choppers in every direction, but they won't know what specifically they're looking for. I'm confident that they won't be on the lookout for the camper van, but I doubt its registration is up to date, so there's a chance that a routine police stop could cause problems. On the other hand, the journey to the mountains will mainly be through rural areas, and Shirley is going to detour around the two towns we need to pass through. The van's top speed is only sixty, so we won't trigger any speed traps, but they will certainly mount roadblocks. I'm unsure how large a radius they'll cover, but roadblocks take time to set up and Sylvie thinks the journey is fairly short, about two and a half hours.

On balance, I think we'll be fine. Staring out of the window at the scenery, I marvel again at what a beautiful country we live in. My eyelids soon feel heavy and, though I try to resist, I'm soon in a deep sleep.

CHAPTER TWENTY-THREE

The *whump-whump* of helicopter blades wakes me with a start. It's dark now, and cloudy, but the chopper's lights are clearly visible as it tracks the highway leading into the first town we need to navigate our way past: Orchard Valley.

"Bad news, Frankie," Shirley says. "The highway is dead straight in this part. There's no way round; we have to go through the town."

"Okay, everyone, stay cool," I say. "If anyone asks, we're just family and friends on a trip to the mountains, okay?" I slip Danny Molinar's gun out of my pocket and hold it ready at my side.

Along its length of about a mile and a half, Orchard Valley has three streets running parallel to each other, connected by three cross streets. It's home to maybe 500 souls. Main Street is well lit but almost deserted, all we see are a few kids outside an ice-cream parlor and a half-empty bar. Nothing more.

There are no signs of a roadblock, but the chopper is keeping pace with us as we trundle along Main Street. Suddenly, I know why.

"Shirl, take the next left and then turn right and follow the road until you find a darkened house, then stop outside as if it is ours," I say urgently.

Bewildered, Shirley signals left and turns calmly. She then turns right onto the road parallel to Main Street.

The chopper follows us.

There are no streetlights, so Shirley slows down slightly and then, about halfway down, pulls into a space outside a house where no lights show. She turns off the engine.

The chopper hovers above us for about thirty seconds then accelerates away.

"What just happened?" Jess says.

"I nearly screwed up, that's what," I answer. "I forgot that Black Ops choppers have infrared imagers fitted. I remembered only when it was tracking us on Main Street. It must have been counting the heat signatures in cars, and we hit the right number, so they took a closer look. You staying so calm made them lose interest, Shirl! After all, five-person families are not uncommon, and when you pulled up outside this dark house, they probably concluded we were just an ordinary family getting home after an evening out."

"Fantastic work, Nanny!" Alex pipes up excitedly. "You should come out of retirement and be a secret agent."

We all laugh at the joke, and the tension lifts.

After a minute, Shirley pulls away again, and we confidently head out of town.

CHAPTER TWENTY-FOUR

At last light, we skirt past Harvest Town without incident. As we begin to climb Starvation Mountain, the fertile plain is quickly replaced by forbidding, rocky terrain. The old VW's engine works hard as the narrow road winds up the mountain in sharp, steep turns. Shirley's knuckles are white as she grips the wheel, but she seems confident and in control, so I'm relaxed and turn my thoughts to our next steps.

Jess says, "It's not too much further now, and in the morning, the view will be worth it. Honestly, it's gorgeous."

About ten minutes later, we see a single-story, sprawling, ranch-style building to our left, reached via a short driveway.

"This is it!" Jess shouts, and Shirley smoothly brings the vehicle to a halt outside the double entrance doors to Starvation Peak Studio – once the inspiration of rockstars, soon to be my confessional booth. Jess taps in the security code, and we all head inside while Shirley parks the van in the garage to the side of the building, out of sight of prying eyes.

As we get inside, the musty place is still in darkness.

Jess calms my rising concern, "The power company must have turned off the service, but there's a generator out back, and Sylvie and Mom are working on it now. We'll be lit soon."

Moments later, fluorescent tube lights illuminate the lobby, and behind a thick glass wall at the back of the room, the studio comes into view.

Alex and I step inside to explore.

CHAPTER TWENTY-FIVE

We enter the studio through sound-proofed double doors. It smells stale, and every surface is covered in dust, but some places hold the imprints of the events they've witnessed, and this place feels consequential. As I think about all the great music recorded here, the hairs on the back of my neck stand up.

To our left is a small control room that overlooks the "live" area where Jess will soon interview me. On three sides, its walls are covered floor to ceiling with the signatures of all the bands who made their albums there. The final wall is covered with signatures up to knee height; the rest of the wall consists of a thick glass window, facing the lobby.

Jess and Sylvie join us. This is their world and they're in control; I'm just following their lead.

"Okay, Mom's seeing what she can make of the food you brought with us," Jess says to me, all business. "So, while she's doing that, let's get a few things set up in the studio, okay?"

"Sure," I reply, unsure what that specifically means but following her into the "live" area anyway.

Sylvie has co-opted Alex to help her move two high-backed, black leather chairs into the center of the room. Between the seats is a low, pine table, which Alex is wiping clean of dust. Above the chairs, microphones hang from the ceiling.

Jess points to the chair on the left and takes the seat opposite. I'm suddenly startled by a flood of light. Sylvie's laugh reverberates around the room, and I twist in my seat to see her sitting up at the control room decks.

"Sorry about that!" Sylvie says over the intercom. "Right, Frankie and Jess, say a few words please."

Jess nods and starts, "The events of the last few weeks have shaken our country to the core. Today, we'll hear from the man responsible." She nods at me to say something.

I'm silent for a moment. The only words that come to my mind are "testing, one, two, three" but, in such an historic place, I want to avoid sounding trite. "My name is Frank Green, Frankie to my friends. Captain Frank Green to the Special Operations Service," I say, evenly.

"Perfect," Sylvie's voice booms. "I'll come down now and check the cameras."

Jess smiles at me, leans across, pats my knee and quietly says, "Relax, you're doing great."

Alex is hovering close by when Sylvie joins us to set the camera up. She looks thoughtfully at him and says, "Alex, wanna try the camera?"

He instantly joins us, keen to learn.

Sylvie says, "Look, I need to be in the control room when the interview happens, so my first idea was to set up the camera in a fixed location. Ideally, though, we'd pan from one person to the other as the speaker changes. There's a skill to it, but it's mainly about keeping your movements slow and steady so the viewer doesn't really notice – we want to make viewers feel like they're in the room with us, moving their own heads as they listen to a conversation. Wanna give it a try?"

Alex nods enthusiastically, and Sylvie shows him the basic camera moves before heading back to the control room.

"Okay, let's go," she says a few moments later. "Short sentences first and remember, smooth and steady, Alex."

This time I start, "I wanted to be a doctor as a kid."

Jess responds, "No way, I did too – that's what my dad was."

"Now longer sentences, please. And again, slow and steady, Alex," Sylvie says.

Jess says, "I didn't get the grades for med school though. Turned out my skills were more in the Arts, but Mom and Dad encouraged me anyway. They always wanted me to follow my own dreams and find something I could work hard at and be proud of. Instead, I chose journalism!"

Alex laughs at the joke, and Sylvie's voice cuts in, "Good, Alex, but you have to remain impassive – when you laughed at your mom's joke, the picture wobbled up and down."

We keep going until Shirley calls us for dinner, but by then Alex is doing well enough to have the job for the live event. I shake his hand, and Jess gives him a huge hug and a sloppy kiss. Sylvie rolls her eyes and laughs happily. After the trauma they've experienced, I'm pleased that the mood in the studio is light and upbeat.

CHAPTER TWENTY-SIX

The positive mood continues over dinner as Shirley tells stories of the scrapes Jess got into as a child. I listen, watch and try to embrace the mood, but I can't help worrying about what could go wrong.

Eventually, I bring the conversation back to why we're here. "What time will we go live, Jess?"

She looks across at Sylvie and says, "I'm thinking we go live at 7am – we'll catch the early birds here, hit lunchtime in Europe and the early evening in Asia."

Sylvie nods at the logic, so I ask my next question. "Once we start, how long will it take for them to shut us down?"

"Short of blowing up all the world's servers, they can't shut us down, Frankie," Sylvie answers. "We're live streaming, and the internet is mightily robust. They could make a dent by disrupting the home-based servers, but the rest of the world will still hear what you say and clips will find their way back over here quickly enough after that. And anyway, we're going to get the message out through a server based in Europe; their only hope of shutting that down is diplomatic pressure, and we'll have finished the broadcast before the politicians have finished their back and forth."

Alex adds, "All true. And the fact is that the internet was designed that way; the Defense Advanced Projects Agency designed it so it could never be shut down." He says this in the matter-of-fact tone of someone who knows they're being clever but wants to appear modest.

Jess and Shirley beam with pride.

I nod in appreciation. "Okay, so, one more question: How long before they figure out where we are once we start broadcasting?"

Sylvie answers, "There's a developer tab on every URL; a skilled technician will unpick it quickly. So, I'd say they'll know where we are early in the broadcast. But as for how quickly they can get here, given where we are, I'd say it'll take some time."

"Okay, so let's aim to get the meat of this out inside thirty minutes, Jess," I say.

Jess says, "We can do that."

We talk for a while longer, but everyone's thoughts drift towards the morning and a chance to make a new piece of Starvation Peak Studio history. With stifled yawns, the group breaks up and, at my insistence, retires to the back of the studios where four double bedrooms are located.

I take my dress uniform out of my rucksack and hang it off a heating pipe in the hope that the creases won't be too obvious in the morning. Then I settle down on an old, brown leather sofa in the back of the studio. It smells like I'm not the first person to have had the idea to sleep there.

***

Sleep is hard to come by. After a couple of hours, I hear the studio door creak slowly open and I'm instantly on my feet.

"It's only me," Jess says softly. "Couldn't sleep."

The sound of her bare feet, soft on the studio floor, tells me she is padding slowly towards me. She shyly places her hands and head on my chest as she reaches me.

"Hold me," she says, a slight catch in her voice.

I wrap her in my arms. Within a minute, she slips her hands under my T-shirt and lifts it over my head, then runs her hands over my body, kissing my skin gently as she explores. I feel myself harden as she unbuckles my belt. Her breathing quickens, then we kiss, long and deep. When we break, Jess slips off her long, black T-shirt and stands naked before me. I hurriedly pull off my jeans and lift her onto my hips. We roll onto the sofa, and she takes me inside her.

Afterwards, we lie wrapped together, our breathing steady and synchronized. Finally, sleep takes us.

CHAPTER TWENTY-SEVEN

When I wake, Jess has already left to prepare for the broadcast, and from the noise and frantic energy around the place, I imagine I'm running late.

I pad bare footed down the hallway to the bathroom at the building's rear, my dress uniform draped over my left arm. When I pass Shirley and Sylvie, they both give me big smiles and knowing looks.

As I turn into the final hallway, I bump into Jess coming out of the room she would have spent the night in if she hadn't spent it with me. I stop in my tracks. She's dressed for TV, and she looks stunning – a short, red jacket over a black, embroidered shirt, and figure-hugging, black jeans. She tilts her head to one side, and the hallway's overhead lights pick out hints of gold in her carefully groomed hair.

"Don't look at me like that," she says, her eyes warm and inviting. "I've done my make-up and I don't want it to crack!"

I kiss her quickly and run towards the showers, shouting back over my shoulder, "I'll be quick!"

She watches me all the way.

CHAPTER TWENTY-EIGHT

"What did you do with Frankie?" Alex asks with a smile when I return to the studio twenty minutes later wearing my dark blue dress uniform, garnered with rows of medal ribbons, and shiny black polished shoes.

Shirley stops what she's doing and looks me up and down, nodding approvingly, just as Jess and Sylvie emerge from the control room and walk towards me.

"Perfect," Sylvie says. "We want everyone to see the long-serving soldier."

I know I cut an imposing figure in my uniform, and I'm proud to wear it. The captain's epaulets on my shoulders and the buttons on my tunic shine, and three rows of medal ribbons above my heart send a clear message about the kind of soldier I am. Or, at least, was.

Jess says, "Okay, Captain Green, one last soundcheck and we'll get this thing rolling."

I'm nervous but excited as Sylvie fits Jess and me with earpieces. When the soundcheck is complete and everyone gives a thumbs up, Jess sits opposite me – we're separated by about eighteen inches; I can smell her perfume, and memories from last night flood in.

As if reading my mind, she winks at me. Then, staring straight into the camera, she begins, "The past few days have been the most extraordinary in our nation's history. It seems like our world had been turned on its head, and the question on everyone's lips has been: Why? Why did this happen? What kind of a monster would do such a thing?

"Well, today we're going to find out. I have with me the man that everyone is looking for. He's a straight talker, so let's get straight to it.

"Captain Frankie Green, why did you kill President Teufel?"

Alex smoothly moves the camera to face me, but I freeze. It's the first time I've heard what I did said out loud, and it's shaken me. The words are stark and don't feel like they fit the man I am, but there is no question – they are the truth.

Jess sees that I'm struggling and hands me a glass of water. "Relax Frankie, in your own time."

I look down, breathe deeply, take a sip of the water and then look directly into the camera. "There are so many reasons why I'm glad he's dead. The conman tricks he played on towns like mine for one: promising a return of the good times, back to prosperity and optimism, but then delivering nothing."

"Good, Frankie, great start," Sylvie says into my earpiece.

Encouraged, I pick up momentum, "When the hope he generated withered, he crushed so many lives. He certainly crushed my mom and dad's. They now lie in Oakvale's cemetery, and I place that firmly at his door!

"But it's more than that. More than the constant lies, the womanizing, the corruption. After all, we knew all that about him when we cast our votes. And to be clear, I did vote for him. Both times."

"So, you voted for him knowing all his faults. What changed?"

I sit up straight and look directly into the camera again. "It became even more personal. I used to do a job for this country. An ugly job. I killed people designated as threats to our nation. I was a Special Forces sniper. That was my job. It's not easy killing someone, and every person I killed scarred me, left a mark on my soul. But I could live with it because it was the right thing to do – the right thing for our country. And let me be clear, I love this country…" My voice shakes with emotion like it always does when I talk about how I feel about this great nation. I take a deep breath, and notice Alex out of the corner of my eye.

Alex's eyes are on his laptop. They are wide and excited, and then his voice is in our earpieces. "We've already gone viral, and not just here – it's the main story in Europe and racing up in Asia fast!"

I try to keep my composure, but that's great news. I look across at Jess who is also struggling to hide her excitement. I have to take this opportunity with both hands. The more people know the truth the better; facing the ugliness of what we've become is the starting point for a better future.

With one more deep breath, I feel more relaxed and the words come more easily. "When I joined up, I just needed a job. Our town's mill had failed, money was short and college was suddenly impossible, so I joined the army. I wanted a trade, something I could use to make a living when I came out, you know? But I excelled on the rifle range, and was told my personality made me a good fit for a sniper – if I believe something is right, I will do it, even if it hurts – so that's the job they trained me for. It was not what I wanted but I believed we were a force for good in the world; so, if my government thought I could best serve the cause as a sniper, then I would do it to the best of my ability.

"So, I buckled down and worked hard. And I was good. Very good. I was in the service for eight years, and I'm proud of the job I did for seven of them. I did as I was ordered; I killed our enemies and kept us all safe."

"So, what happened?" Jess asks, leaning forward in her seat.

"Teufel was re-elected as President is what happened, and then the brakes came off." I feel my throat tighten as I speak, and although I'm trying hard to stay calm, I can hear the anger in my voice, barely suppressed. I take a moment, then continue, "His critics always said that if he was re-elected, he'd mold the country to serve his needs, not adapt himself to serve the country's. I didn't believe them, but I'm here to tell you now that I was wrong."

Sylvie comes through in my earpiece, "Frankie, there's movement on the road outside. We don't know what it is yet. I'll come back shortly, but it might be smart to speed things up, just in case."

Jess and I exchange puzzled looks, but I get to the point anyway.

"I only learned by accident, but the fact is that since he came back to office, my missions have been in support of Teufel's interests, not our nation's. The last people I killed were *not* our nation's enemies, they were just in Teufel's way."

Jess quickly follows up, "So, how did they get in the way?"

"Simple – they opposed one of Teufel's business deals, a part of his corporate expansion plan, so they needed to go. Teufel had me do it. I killed men who I thought were our enemies, but all they did was to say no to a Teufel deal. He turned me into his own personal assassin, like a Mob hitman. And I could not live with that."

CHAPTER TWENTY-NINE

I pause and look across at Jess. Her eyes are wide and she's momentarily lost her composure. I've unwittingly shocked and wrong-footed her.

Alex looks lost too, but Sylvie chimes in, confident and in control, "Jess, get a grip. Alex, camera on your mom."

"That's a big claim," Jess says, quickly improvising. "How can you be certain?"

A loud, rumbling noise somewhere outside the building captures our attention. I see Shirley run out of the studio and peer through the window next to the main doors – just a quick glance before going into the control room.

After Shirley has had a brief conversation with Sylvie, we hear Sylvie in our earpieces, "There's a crowd gathering out there. They're not army, although some do have weapons. They're coming up the hill from the town we came through; their trucks and cars have already blocked the road, and they look angry. Hard to say how many, maybe twenty so far."

Jess and I look at each other, weighing up our options, but then Sylvie makes up our minds for us.

"Keep rolling guys," she says. "I'm not going to break the feed; we might not get it back."

I nod my understanding but I'm stunned by the speed of what's happened. I'm not surprised that the crowd is angry – this is Teufel's heartland after all – but I am astonished that they found us so quickly. I have no idea how they could have worked out where we are.

Then, Alex peers out from behind the camera, eyebrows raised. Shaking his head in frustration, he points at the wall between us. "Look, down there. They know because we told them."

Jess and I look down at the half-wall next to us, from which the soundproof glass rises, and immediately understand what's happened. One signature stands out among the many covering the wall: *Starvation Peak – already so high, you don't need drugs*, followed by the four signatures of the 1980s chart-topping band, Halogen Monkeys.

I glance at Jess who flops back in her seat, deflated. "We're screwed," she says.

My mind is whirring, but I don't see it that way. The good news is that the crowd outside is not Black Ops – couldn't possibly be based on what Sylvie said – and with a crowd already here, Black Ops won't make an appearance – too public. And anyway, their mission was to stop me talking and they've failed to do that. I suspect that it's townsfolk out there, but law enforcement will certainly follow soon, so we don't have much time. And I have more to say.

I look pleadingly at Jess and say, "Let's keep going, okay?"

After a moment's reflection, she sits up straight and leans forward. The determined girl I knew all those years ago is back! Alex smiles widely and turns the camera on his mom.

"Like I said, Frankie, you've made a big claim but how do you know for sure that you're right?"

With my right hand, I reach into my uniform's inside pocket and extract a single sheet of folded paper. It is cream in color, smooth and thick – high quality. At the top of the page is the President's seal.

I hold it up to the camera and explain, "Listed on this paper are eight names. All are now dead because Teufel ordered them so. Next to each name is a tick in blue ink; the last tick was made by the VP when I confirmed the final kill."

"The VP, you mean President Teufel's son?" Jess says, now fully engaged again.

I nod. "That's right – Teufel turned government into a family business."

"So, what did these eight people have in common that made them the President's enemies?"

I laugh bitterly. "These men were a group of powerful, middle eastern sheiks who blocked a development Teufel wanted to build in their country – the only country in the region who always said 'no'. To be clear, these were not 'good men'. They operated in the shadows of their country's economy, but the only thing they ever did to get on the wrong side of Teufel was oppose his deal."

I pause and swallow hard. Jess leans forward and nods encouragingly. I don't want to say out loud what I have to say next, but I must.

"Truth is," I say quietly, my voice tight with anger, and tears of frustration moistening my eyes as I stare straight at the camera, "he had me kill eight men and ruin the lives of those who loved them so he could build another damned golf course!"

I hold up the sheet of paper to the camera, closer this time so it will be easy for viewers to read, and steady so anyone wanting to take a screenshot will get a clear image. Above the list of eight Arabic names on the President's official paper, the memo's headline reads: *Those voting against the proposed development of Rub' Al Khalif by the Stallion Golf Group.* I'm confident that people will recognize Teufel's company name and then scurry to validate the Presidential seal and check the names on the list. I carefully fold the paper and put it back in my jacket pocket.

Just then, the front door to the studio bursts open, and men and women waving batons, axes and guns flood in.

CHAPTER THIRTY

Access to the live studio and its control room is through a keypad, so, without the code, the mob resorts to banging on the door and soundproof window, faces contorted with rage. It's scary, but I glance at Jess, Alex and Shirley, who is now standing just behind Alex with her hands on his shoulders, and see they all look scared but resolute.

Then Sylvie, all cool professionalism, says into our earpieces, "Keep going. That's toughened glass; they won't get in quickly. I'm going to feed your conversation out to the lobby so they can hear what you two say. It might calm some of them down to know what really happened."

"Is that wise?" I ask.

"Trust me, Frankie," Sylvie quickly responds. "Alex, find an angle that includes the crowd, Frankie and your mom. We'll keep the broadcast going."

Alex chimes in excitedly, "It's viral everywhere, guys!" He changes position slightly to capture the angry faces behind me, baying for my blood.

I look at Jess questioningly. If she wants to bail out, we'll shut the broadcast down. She looks anxious but nods to continue and moves to the edge of her seat.

With her professional composure gone, the words tumble out of her mouth, but they are the right questions to ask all the same, "So, what happened, Frankie? How'd you get the paper? How did he die? Did you shoot him?"

I pause before I answer, trying to ignore the sounds of fury on the other side of the glass. "No, I didn't shoot him. I had no weapons…" I am momentarily distracted by the echo created by the simultaneous broadcast to the lobby. "It's part of the protocol, even for senior military leaders; you're never armed when you meet the President.

"When I'd met him previously, it was always in a sterile, controlled environment at the Big House, at carefully managed award ceremonies for killing our enemies. But he was really keen to know the outcome of this one. I only knew he was at the base when I stepped off the plane – the base CO took me to one side and said the President was there and wanted to see me. I was surprised but followed the CO's direction.

"But when I entered the hangar, the VP was there, not President Teufel."

I glance to my right. The lobby is now full of people, but they are no longer shouting. Most are listening, some are watching the feed live on their cell phones.

Relieved, I continue, "It was weird, the VP didn't even exchange pleasantries, he just seemed really agitated. Didn't even wait for me to reach him but shouted across the hangar: 'Tell me you got him!' When I nodded to confirm that I did, he briefly fist-pumped the air and marked a piece of paper he was holding in his left hand – the one I just showed everyone.

"Just then, a member of the President's security team stuck his head through the side door and bellowed, 'Hey Junior, the boss needs you out here, like NOW!' The VP seemed suddenly flustered, a little scared even. He hurriedly folded the paper and attempted to slip it into his inside suit jacket pocket as he rushed to the door, but the paper somehow ended up on the floor. I saw it straight away and called after him, but he was in too much of a hurry to listen, so I picked it up, intending to give it to him when he came back."

Jess says, "So, at that point you looked at the note?"

"Yes. I normally would not even have dreamt of doing that, but his behavior was so odd I was intrigued. So, I opened it, and the pieces fell into place as soon as I recognized the last two names – they were both people I had killed in the last six months."

I glance at the mob in the lobby. They're quiet now, just a few murmurs of conversation.

Jess gently asks, "How did that make you feel?"

"Disgusted, outraged, sick to the stomach." I abruptly stop, my body flooded with the nauseating memory of that moment.

Taking a deep breath, I continue, "Less than a minute later, the door opened. I heard raised voices in the background, and then Teufel strode out, all swagger. His bodyguards were right behind him, but he waved them back, saying, 'Stay with Junior, he needs all the help he can get, the fucking loser. I'm fine here.'"

I hear cheers from the studio lobby. They like the way Teufel talks. They say he "keeps it real."

I continue, "Teufel strode over to me, a burger in his right hand and a Diet Coke in his left and said, 'Gotta love our military bases, every one of them has a burger joint.' Then he juggled his burger into his left hand and held out his right for me to shake. I didn't take it."

I hear a chorus of angry shouts from the lobby, but I block them out.

"I was calm by this point, a cold, steely feeling had settled on me, like it did on my missions. I said to the President, 'Surely no golf club is worth a single life, let alone so many,' and held up the sheet of paper the VP had dropped.

"Teufel shrugged and looked at me quizzically, then he took another bite of his burger, and chewed as he spoke, 'I don't know what the fuck you're talking about, son, and I don't like your tone. Show some respect!'"

Another cheer from the studio lobby followed.

"So, I continued and laid out what I knew. I said, 'You had me kill men so you could build a fucking golf course. You expect me to respect that?' He fixed me with an intense stare, took another bite of his burger and a slurp of his drink, and attempted to wave it off, like it was no big deal. 'Aw, come on kid, grow up. They were just a bunch of ragheads, no use to anyone. And you can't stop progress, right?' He opened his arms wide then and beamed that million-watt smile his followers love so much."

More cheers from the lobby.

I wait for them to subside and continue, "Then the famous Teufel smile disappeared, and he was all business. He said, 'Okay, so, how much? How much to keep your mouth shut?'"

Alex now has the camera fixed firmly on me, so I look directly into it.

"I didn't respond. In that moment, I hated him with an intensity I'd never felt before – to think that I could be bought! He represented everything ugly our great nation has become. And I snapped. I punched him in the gut. Just once, but hard. A fit man would have been winded and recovered, but Teufel was not fit, he had no muscle tone and, to make matters worse, he'd just taken another mouthful of burger. He should have spat it out, but he closed his mouth instead, then quickly ran out of air. As he sucked air in, he sucked in pieces of the burger."

There's a low hum in the lobby. I glance at Jess, who looks confused, but I'm not sure why.

"Perhaps I could have saved him then, could have performed the Heimlich maneuver immediately. You know, squeezed his ribs, made him cough up his burger. But at that moment, I wanted him to suffer for the pain he put Oakvale through, the pain he caused my parents with the false hope he kindled, and for turning me into nothing more than a low-life gangster, a hitman. And he did suffer; his face quickly went red, veins burst in his already flushed face; his eyes pleaded as he gasped and reached towards me for help, like a baby, sobbing and begging. He weakened quickly and sank to his knees. Terrified, he grabbed my legs and reached up to me – he even wet himself."

I glance to my right again and scan the faces in the crowd. Some look furious, but many more are looking awkwardly at their feet like they're embarrassed to imagine their great leader in such a state.

Jess's voice brings me back to the moment. "So, he choked to death?"

I nod and continue evenly, "He was so fat, so unfit, and despite the big lie that he was the fittest President ever, he evidently had a heart condition. His body only experienced a brief trauma, but his heart couldn't take it; he went into cardiac arrest. His last breath was a whimper."

Jess sits back in her seat and lets out a long breath of air. "Frankie, I'm no lawyer but I don't think what you've described is murder, and it's certainly not what the authorities have told us you did."

The lobby is completely quiet now.

I stand, turn to face them and say as clearly as I can through my quavering voice, "Look, I get that you're angry. I get that you hate me for what I did. And I own it. No matter how you dress it up, I killed President Teufel that day just as much as if I had used my sniper rifle.

"I know I have to pay for it – probably with my life – and if that's what a court decides, then so be it. I have been chased for days by government operatives trying to deny me the chance to explain what happened, but you all need to know. Actually, the entire world needs to know. And now it's out there."

I scan the crowd. Some look like they'd like to lynch me, many look sad and thoughtful, a few hold my gaze and nod a kind of grudging respect.

I take another sip of water and glance down at Jess who mouths, "Well done."

I help her to her feet, hug her tight and whisper, "Thank *you*," into her ear.

The sense of relief is enormous. It's out there now for everyone to dissect, analyze and factcheck. Whatever happens next, the world knows the truth. It feels good.

Then the police arrive.

CHAPTER THIRTY-ONE

A cacophony of sirens tells me they've come in force. Ten officers race into the lobby, guns drawn. The crowd parts to let them through.

I raise my hands, facing the on-rushing officers, and shout to Shirley to unlock the studio. Sylvie, Jess, Alex and Shirley all come stand next to me with their hands raised.

I look at each of them and say, "Thank you!"

They just smile back and nod.

Then, Alex pipes up, a cheeky grin on his face, "I left the camera running."

Sylvie adds mischievously, "Oh, and by the way, we're still broadcasting to the world." Then whispers, "I shut down the feed to the lobby, though."

Despite everything, a smile cracks my face and I clap to them all. "You guys are the absolute best."

Then the first officers enter the studio and the mood changes quickly.

"On the floor facedown, mother fuckers. Arms behind your backs."

We do as instructed, and handcuffs snap tightly on our wrists.

I look up at the officer in front of me, a guy in his mid-thirties, tall, thick around the middle but strong looking. His eyes are set closely together and he has thick, bushy black eyebrows and a crew cut.

I say, "Guys, come on. It's me you're here for, these people have done nothing – let them go."

"Shut the fuck up," he replies and stamps on my head, his heavy soled tactical boot glancing off my temple.

A wave of nausea washes over me, my vision narrows to a dot. Then, blackness.

PART TWO

CHAPTER THIRTY-TWO

As consciousness returns in blurry waves, my senses are assaulted: cold, urine and dampness make me gag and force my head up from the floor; my eyes are gritty; my mouth feels like someone wiped the moisture out of it.

Slowly, things come into focus. A narrow window at the top of one wall provides limited natural light, and a single lightbulb hanging from the center of the room provides enough additional light to see by. In one corner, a battered metal bucket appears to be the origin of the urine smell; in the opposite the corner, a white porcelain sink, stained by age and neglect, sits below a dripping tap. Grimy, white-tiled walls and a concrete floor with decades of dirt ground into it complete the picture.

Then, a pair of expensive-looking, brown brogues come into view, polished to a bright shine. I strain to follow the line of the tailored trousers, green flecked with brown, that rise above the shoes. I push myself onto my left side to get a better look at the owner.

Everything hurts. Panting, I try to get up, but I'm too weak and settle for shuffling backwards and sitting with my back against the cell wall. I squint and follow the sharp trouser crease from the brogues up over an expensive belt and tie to a slight double chin and a pleasant-looking, middle-aged face with high cheekbones.

The man hands me a cup of water as he speaks, "Ah, good, good. I was getting a little worried about you," in an accent I can't quite place. He leans down and offers me a hand. "I'm Adam Sinclair."

He hauls me up and guides me to a narrow bed pushed against the wall on the left-hand side of the room. It's covered in a single dirty white sheet and a misshapen pillow. It's just three steps away, but the effort is all-consuming.

I flop down, breathing heavily. Sinclair remains standing.

"Look, take a moment. I'd drink the water if I was you – I should think you're very dehydrated," he says.

The water is cold and reviving. My head clears sufficiently to take the man in properly. He's about five feet eight inches tall, stocky and handsome. His graying, thick brown hair is neatly trimmed, and behind gold-rimmed spectacles, kind eyes sparkle with intelligence.

"Look, I'm afraid we don't have much time, so forgive me if I get down to business. I'm the court appointed defense; *your* court appointed defense."

I finally place the accent. "You're English?"

"Good catch," Sinclair says, chuckling, "Yes, born and bred, but I've been over here a long time and, most importantly, I learned the law here, Frankie." He hesitates and then says, "May I call you Frankie? I don't like to presume."

Although it hurts, I smile and nod. I like this guy.

"It took me an age to find you in this labyrinthine system, and even when I did it took me another twenty-four hours to secure access," Sinclair says.

"Wait. What? So, how long ago was I arrested?"

"Three days," he replies flatly. "And by the looks of you, it's been three days of beatings – although nobody will ever admit it. It's astonishing how often prisoners fall down stairs in this place!"

I laugh but quickly stop – stabbing pains in my ribs take my breath away.

When the pain subsides, I ask, "And where is this place? I mean, it's obviously a prison but—"

"Of course, of course. Silly of me. We're in a maximum-security prison called The Sentinel. It's in the capital, close to the courts. Look," he says, a determined expression on his face, "we need to get you checked over by a doctor and moved somewhere more sanitary, then we can start planning. We need to work quickly; your first court appearance is on Friday."

I must look shocked because he quickly adds, "Don't worry, it'll be brief, just the charges and your plea, then back to your cell. Even so, we do need to prepare."

"When's Friday?"

"Two days from now," Sinclair says, his eyebrows raised in surprise. "I can see they really did a number on you, Frankie. Do you remember anything at all from the last few days?"

I look down and try to gather my thoughts, then shake my head. "No, not really."

Stifling a look of outrage, Sinclair continues, "They're pushing for a quick trial, Frankie. They want you dealt with and out of the way so the VP can be sworn in and move on with his agenda. Or, more accurately, his father's agenda. We can assume there will be no change – like father like son, eh?" Sinclair smirks, pleased with himself, but I don't respond. "Anyway, given the circumstances, there's very little I can do to slow them down."

I stare at the cell floor and mull his last comment over, then nod my understanding. "What about everyone else? Are they okay?"

"They are for now. All released and bailed. But they face serious charges – obstructing justice." My heart sinks, but Sinclair leans in and adds, "Look, given the ambiguity over what they knew and when, and the fact that Sylvie and Jess have journalistic privilege, I doubt they'll do time. If anything, it'll be a show trial. The spotlight is firmly on you, Frankie. It's you they want to make an example of."

"What's the charge?" I ask, feeling oddly detached from whatever answer comes.

Sinclair hesitates. "Look, you need to know what you're up against, but I don't want you to worry, okay? We are going to fight this hard and we have some good challenges to run with."

"I get it, but, Mr. Sinclair, to get the best out of me, you need to know never to treat me with kid gloves. Please, just tell me how it is, okay. I *will* handle it." I feel weary but immediately regret the irritation in my voice.

Sinclair stares at me long and hard, sighs and looks down before saying, quietly, "We'll discuss it more fully when we meet to plan the hearing, but the charge is first-degree murder." He holds his hands up as if to fend me off. "It's unprecedented. The facts of your case *might* fit the fact pattern for *second*-degree murder, but they are attempting to re-write the law in a hurry."

Sinclair relaxes when he realizes that I'm calm about the news, then I ask, genuinely curious, "Surely, they can't do that, right? I mean the law is the law! They can't just invent new ones, on a whim!"

He nods but still looks concerned. "You're right, Frankie. The idea is preposterous. Or, rather, it should be. I'd certainly have been kicked out of law school for even suggesting such a thing, but Teufel's second term has been marked by so many unprecedented changes that I must admit I am concerned that they'll get away with it!" Sinclair looks at me appraisingly for a moment, then says, "You've asked me to be completely open with you, Frankie. You should also know that the judge, Judge Longyear, is a Teufel appointee. He is ambitious and he has his sights set on the Top Court. I fear he'll see a career opportunity in being the judge who deals with Teufel's killer harshly." Hesitating, he looks me in the eyes, his soft brown irises alive with indignation. "And they want the death penalty."

I'm not surprised; it's what I expected. But the words still feel like a punch to the solar plexus.

A loud thumping on the door is accompanied by a shout, "Time's up."

Sinclair bites his lip in anger and mutters to himself, "Outrageous!" Gathering his things together, he says, "No point in me getting on their wrong side, too. Look, we'll meet tomorrow and plan properly, just try not to worry, okay?"

I nod agreement, but as soon as the cell door closes behind him, my mind races. I was raised to face the consequences of my actions, and I'm ready to do that – we are a country of laws, and I will face whatever the law says I should face. But laws made on the hoof to suit the agenda of whoever is in power is just plain wrong. It's *not* how I was raised, it's not right, it's not who we are as a nation, *it's not what I killed to defend.*

A scream suddenly erupts from my throat, loud and angry. The pain in my ribs is crippling, it bends me double. But I can't stop.

CHAPTER THIRTY-THREE

I'm taken to the medical unit an hour after Sinclair leaves, where a disinterested doctor checks me over then issues treatment orders to a severe-looking, elderly nurse in a tightly fitting blue uniform. I'm calmer now, but my mind is on the trial not the medical diagnosis and I don't take in what the doctor tells her.

When he leaves, the nurse orders me into a shower in the corner of the surgery. On my way, I pass a wall mirror that shows me what the last few days in custody have cost my body: I'm heavily bruised from head to toe, my nose is broken, there are black rings around both of my eyes and my lips are cracked and scabbed. I feel as bad as I look.

The hot water washing over me is refreshing, and I gingerly wash my hair and body before carefully drying myself and emerging from the shower.

The nurse is waiting. She orders me to sit and immediately wraps bandages tightly around my ribs. In a voice much softer than her austere appearance led me to expect, she explains, "Three cracked ribs, I'm afraid, and you know about your nose. The rest is bruising. But we need to monitor your kidneys – there's blood in your urine. The doctor expects it will be fine in a couple of days, but if it's not we'll need to take a closer look. We'll check again on Friday."

"I'm in court on Friday," I say, wincing as she pulls the bandages tighter.

The nurse can't hide her surprise, but she recovers quickly. "Okay, we'll try to fit it in before you leave for court then. If not, Saturday will have to do. For now, rest as much as you can, okay?"

I nod and shuffle back to my cell, a heavy-set guard prodding me in the kidneys with his billy stick all the way.

The bed sheets smell of stale sweat. I strip them off and toss them into a corner. The limited daylight provided by the narrow window at the top of the wall is gone; it's dark outside. I drink a cup of water and lie down to rest.

It seems like five minutes later that a guard hammers on my cell door. I glance up and know that I've slept for hours; the narrow window is bright with daylight again.

I stand and straighten slowly. It hurts a little less, but it still hurts.

CHAPTER THIRTY-FOUR

I attempt to engage the guard in conversation as he puts cuffs on my wrists, but he ignores my efforts and, without saying a word, points down the hallway with his billy stick and nods for me to walk.

I'm still stiff, but my shuffle has become a limp. Regular prods to my kidneys keep me moving along the faded, red-polished concrete floors that line the prison's gray-walled hallways. We pass rows of cell doors whose window coverings have been drawn back by the guards. Pale faces desperate for human contact peer out and shout across the hallway. Other inmates immediately respond.

We pass through two security checkpoints staffed with armed guards, whose cold-eyed expressions leave me in no doubt what they'd like to do to me.

Eventually, we emerge into a brightly lit lobby. The contrast with the cell block is stark; it has thick, red carpet, a large vase of fresh flowers at its center, and there are four meeting rooms with heavy oak doors spaced around the perimeter.

Sinclair is waiting at the door of the meeting room facing the hallway I emerge from. He looks anxious.

The guard prods me over to him then abruptly turns to stand guard.

"Cuffs!" Sinclair yells, his voice full of aggression.

The guard turns back slowly, a haughty sneer on his face, and roughly unlocks my handcuffs.

Sinclair stares at the guard as he closes the door and mutters, still angry, "Fucking barbarian."

The guard stifles a laugh, turns his back on Sinclair and resumes his guard duties. Sinclair shuts the door fully and rests his back against it, looking as though he might reopen it and punch the guard. But the moment passes, and when he turns to me, he's calm and engaging again.

"How are you?" he says.

"Okay, I guess. Considering."

"Help yourself to coffee and pastries," Sinclair says, nodding towards a side table on which stands a coffee pot and a plate full of croissants.

While I help myself, Sinclair slips off his jacket, rolls up his sleeves and then takes the seat at the head of the table. He places an elegant-looking fountain pen on a yellow legal pad in front of him and waits for me to settle.

I sit on Sinclair's right side and take a deep draft of the coffee. It tastes fresh, and its rich aromas flood my nose. The croissant is delicious, and I'm suddenly aware that I'm very hungry – I can't recall the last time I ate.

The look on my face must reveal how I'm feeling because Sinclair says, "Have as many as you like, Frankie. I got them for you." He pats his slightly bulging stomach and adds with a laugh, "I don't need any more calories!"

His kindness makes me smile, and I help myself to another pastry.

Sinclair begins. "First of all, this is a confidential conversation, Frankie. The room is soundproof and there are no hidden microphones. I know – I checked! Tomorrow, we'll be in court; not for the trial, just for charges to be laid and your plea to be entered, okay?"

I nod, my mouth full.

"They have one charge, and the judge will ask you for your plea. I'm going to run through how I imagine things playing out. Ask any questions as we go, okay?"

Still chewing my pastry, I nod again.

"Before we start, I have an update for you on Jess and the rest of the crew, and for once I have good news. All charges have been dropped!"

Almost spitting crumbs everywhere, I give a brief whoop and lean forward to hear the details.

"As I thought, the journalistic privilege provided a shield for Jess and Sylvie, and Alex is too young. Shirley is too old for them to bother with. Time spent prosecuting them would have resulted in nothing more than fines or suspended sentences, but they want blood, and you're their only hope of satisfying that craving."

My spirits lifted, I'm ready to focus fully on my own case.

Sinclair picks up the signs and says, "Alright, as I mentioned, tomorrow you will be charged with the first-degree murder of President Teufel. I will object – they cannot prove intent and planning, and that's crucial for a first-degree murder charge. And there's a video of the whole thing." Indignation rises in his voice. "It clearly shows that you reacted to something Teufel said and hit him, he fell ill and subsequently died. It's clear. That's a second-degree murder charge at most, not first-degree."

I take a moment to process this information then say, "A video?"

"Yes, CCTV. It was the devil of a job to get a copy – and it's probably better that you don't know precisely how I got it – the key thing, though, is that I have a copy. Which is why it's so perplexing that the prosecution is going with the first-degree murder charge. They have access to the video too, so they know what it shows and they therefore know that the judge must reject their charge and tell them to think again. Obviously, they want first-degree so they can have you executed; with second-degree that's not an option, life is the maximum outcome. If they win."

"Well, there's really no doubt is there? That's what happened, so my plea is guilty," I say calmly. "I did what I did. The President died because of what I did, so I deserve whatever the law says I deserve, right?"

Sinclair leans back in his seat, eyebrows raised, then his booming laugh fills the room.

"No, Frankie. Not right!" He steadies himself. "First of all, what you did was not first-degree murder, and even with second-degree there were extenuating circumstances. You were provoked, you reacted, and that makes a difference. Sure, if you'd hit Teufel without provocation there'd be no debate, but you didn't – he did provoke you. I've seen the footage, and while I don't know what he said in the hangar – there's no sound with the video – it plainly upset you. And I've watched your broadcast where you told the world the full story. Honestly, in the circumstances, I think they'll have a hard time proving even second-degree."

"So, what do I say when the judge reads out the charge?"

"Not guilty! Say it loud and clear, Frankie."

Sinclair is only doing his job, but can't I do what he asks. Teufel is dead because of me. I deserve to be punished according to the law!

Before I can speak, Sinclair leans forward, reaches across the table and places his right hand on my arm. "Frankie, I can tell that you're uncomfortable and I think I know why. I've read your service record, I know your family history, and I know the kind of community you grew up in. I really do. But life is never black and white, and this case is most definitely not. Please enter a not guilty plea and let the justice system do its work, okay? The system is adversarial by design; you should enter a not guilty plea and force the prosecutors to make their case while I defend you. Then let a jury of your peers determine the outcome, okay? It's how the system works. Let it do its job."

I'm still not comfortable but I see his point and nod my agreement.

A thought suddenly comes to mind. "The list. Did you get the list? The list of people Teufel had killed so he could build his golf course?"

Sinclair briefly hesitates. "I haven't actually seen the list, Frankie, but it is noted on the list of items collected from you when you were arrested at the studio, so I think we can assume it's secure. Things are moving fast now though, and we'll definitely need it."

He makes a note on a growing list of 'Things to Do."

CHAPTER THIRTY-FIVE

I don't see the outside world on my way to the courthouse the next morning. I'm taken through a warren of underground hallways to a loading dock where a dark blue van with blacked-out windows awaits.

Two burly guards bundle me into the back of the van. One handcuffs my feet to my seat, which is flush against the side of the van, while the other cuffs my hands in front of me. I don't resist.

The guards then strap themselves into their seats, facing forward, and we set off. They talk quietly to one another throughout the journey; I think through how the next two hours might go and try to remain calm.

Twenty minutes later, we head down a steep slope and come to a sudden stop. The cuffs are removed from my legs, but my hands remain secured. I'm removed from the van, and I see that we're under what I assume is the courthouse.

Two uniformed guards are waiting for me. They usher me into a brightly lit tunnel that runs underneath the building, and after a short walk, we reach a bank of elevators. One guard steps into an elevator ahead of me, and the other follows me in. I'm sandwiched between them for the three floors we ascend before coming to a halt.

The elevator doors open onto a pink-marble-floored atrium. A huge chandelier hangs from a carved-stone ceiling rose thirty feet above us, lighting the space as brightly as if we were outside.

Sinclair is waiting for me. His shoulders are hunched and he's looking down, muttering something under his breath that I can't make out. He stops when I approach and again insists that the guards uncuff me.

They reluctantly comply, and Sinclair leads me into a side room.

"Take a seat, Frankie," he says, his voice calm.

He remains standing, the nervous tension I saw in the atrium gone. He looks ready, and he cuts a dashing figure in a smart, three-piece suit with a gold chain threading down into a waist-coat pocket, out of which he extracts a gold watch.

Glancing at it briefly, he says, "Ten minutes to go. Okay, so, as we discussed, today you should say nothing except to confirm your name, and when asked, plead not guilty, okay?"

"Right," I reply.

Then Sinclair puts his hands on the table and leans forward, looking me squarely in the eyes. "Things could get a little testy in there today, Frankie. Something is very off, and I may need to behave badly to force the issue out into the open. I'm not going to share the details of my suspicions with you now, I just want you to be aware that I have them. And above all, I want you NOT to get upset, okay?"

I smile to myself – what I think of as "behaving badly" is probably very different from Sinclair's idea of it. I can't imagine this kindly, mild-mannered man doing or saying anything that would shock me, but I agree to manage my reactions anyway.

Satisfied, Sinclair pushes himself upright and straightens his tie.

Moments later, when a knock at the door signals that it's our turn in court, he says, "Okay, we go in through different entrances. I'll see you in there." Then he shakes my hand and adds, "Remember, stay calm."

***

Back in the Atrium, Sinclair turns right and enters the courtroom through intricately carved, varnished oak double doors. I'm led to the left, down a short flight of stairs and then underneath the atrium to another short set of steps leading up into the courtroom.

At the top of the steps, I emerge into a low wooden box set to the right of the court and raised up. There's a simple wooden seat, but I remain standing. The room is full, and I'm suddenly acutely aware that I'm visible from every part of it – and all eyes are on me, as well as the media's cameras. There's a flurry of chatter and fingers pointed in my direction. I feel awkward; I'm not used to being in the spotlight, and I don't like it.

I drop my gaze to the floor and continue to stand when Judge Longyear enters. From the corner of my eye, I can see he's well-dressed, tall and slightly hunched with graying hair.

Longyear calls the court to order. Once the room quietens down, he says, "We are here today to hear charges brought against the defendant, Frank Green, for the killing of President Teufel, and to hear his plea. Who speaks for the prosecution?"

A tall, dapper-looking man in his mid-fifties, with thinning sandy-colored hair, stands and languidly steps out from behind one of the two desks at the front of the courtroom facing the judge. Sinclair remains seated at the other desk.

"I will lead the prosecution, Your Honor. Christopher J. Zimmerman," the man says confidently.

"It's nice to see you again, Mr. Zimmerman. What is the charge?" Judge Longyear asks.

"It's very good to be in your courtroom again, Judge Longyear. First-degree murder is the charge," Zimmerman says with a flourish, turning to face me as he finishes, a flash of mockery in his eyes.

There are a few gasps of surprise around the court, which is suddenly full of chatter.

That abruptly ends when Sinclair jumps to his feet. He strides out to the front of the courtroom and puts his hands on his hips. When he speaks, his voice shakes with anger.

"That is absurd, Your Honor. You must reject the charge and advise Mr. Zimmerman to revise his Law 101 class. The charge he has brought simply does not fit the facts of the case."

Zimmerman ignores Sinclair and cockily waves at someone he knows in the press gallery. Judge Longyear languidly scratches his double chin then pushes his gold-rimmed spectacles higher up his nose and replies coldly, "Mr. Sinclair, never advise me again on what I should and should not do in my court, or I will hold you in contempt.

"And on the matter you raise, it is you who needs educating. At this very moment, the Top Court is deliberating a change to the law, an exception to cover cases in which a member of Cabinet is killed while serving. The proposition is that, in such cases, a charge of first-degree murder must be brought. I expect it to become law before the day is out, so I am happy to accept Mr. Zimmerman's charge."

There are audible gasps from around the courtroom.

Sinclair starts to pace as I saw him doing in the atrium, his head down. Then he lifts his head and stops, facing into the courtroom, his back to the judge, and responds – and I finally understand why he saw fit to prepare me. "Actually, Your Honor, I did hear this news late last evening, on the grapevine. But I assumed it was no more than absurd gossip. After all, I *assumed*, with something as consequential as this, that you would have informed me as soon as you knew." Sinclair's voice is laden with sarcasm as he turns to face Longyear. "I would very much have preferred to hear it from you before reaching court, Judge Longyear. It would have been a simple courtesy – not too much to ask, surely."

The judge looks uncomfortable but, before he can speak, Sinclair continues, turning to face the court again, his voice rising and his English accent becoming even more pronounced as his anger rises.

"Be that as it may, what you are advising me, just for the clarity of the press and the members of the public who have chosen to be with us today, is that we as a country have fallen so low that we will now *change settled law just to suit the whims of a useful political outcome. It's a DISGRACE!"*

Longyear slams his hand down on his desk and shouts, "Enough! Stop there, Sinclair. Be very careful what you say next."

Sinclair raises his shoulders in a shrug towards the press gallery and turns back to face the judge, his expression loaded with contempt. "Your Honor, there is no other explanation. As I will show in the course of this trial, the government tried very hard to silence my client before his arrest. He was in possession of facts deeply embarrassing to the President, and for that they tried to kill him."

Sinclair strides over to the public gallery and speaks directly to them. "Ladies and gentlemen, the prosecution are trying to bury the last of the evidence of President Teufel's corruption! That is precisely what this trial is: an attempt to paper over the cracks of a system that's turned its back on democracy. I want to be very clear, Mr. Green's life matters, of course it does, but the outcome of this trial matters even more for the survival of this rapidly declining nation. If corruption wins, then we are all doomed!"

Judge Longyear bangs his gavel continuously, shouting at Sinclair to stop.

But Sinclair is not finished. He turns to face the judge and shouts, "If we bend the law to suit the demands of our leaders then we are nothing more than a tinpot dictatorship!"

The court descends into chaos with the press peppering the judge with questions and angry shouts from the public gallery.

Judge Longyear bangs his gavel again and calls over the din, "This court is adjourned. Mr. Zimmerman, Sinclair, meet me in my chambers. NOW!"

CHAPTER THIRTY-SIX

I'm led back to the meeting room below the court to stew, but I don't have to wait long for Sinclair to join me. I was expecting him to be flustered and angry but he's surprisingly calm as he enters the room and, without speaking, takes the seat opposite me where he sits quietly, staring at the ceiling.

He's lost in thought, so I try to be patient, but after a couple of minutes I break the silence. "You okay?"

"Hmm, what?" Sinclair finally brings his gaze down from the ceiling to look at me. "Oh, yes, I'm very well, thank you. I was just running through things in my mind and, on reflection, I don't think it could have gone any better today."

I don't know what to say. It seemed like a disaster to me.

Sinclair studies me carefully, then a warm smile spreads across his face and he reaches across and pats my arm. "Don't worry, Frankie. Everything's on track. They attempted to blindside me today, you know, about the change of law thing, but I got a call from a journalist late last night who tipped me off – an old pal from university who did the decent thing – thought I should know. So, I had time to prepare my speech."

"Wait, what? You're saying what you did in there was rehearsed?"

He looks at me slyly, humor lighting his dark brown eyes. "Oh yes, dear boy, very much so. It was designed to puncture the arrogance of Longyear, Zimmerman and their cronies, and to get us on the front pages of tomorrow's papers. We'll see what happens, but I think we've achieved that."

I laugh out loud but immediately regret it when shockwaves of pain shoot through my ribs.

"And sorry for not letting you in on it before we went in. I needed them to see that you were as stunned as everyone else was, so I couldn't alert you fully to what was coming. And you certainly did look stunned!"

"I was. Completely," I say. "So, what happened in the judge's chambers? He looked mad as hell."

"Yes, he was, or, I should say, still is and will likely remain so for a while yet. I embarrassed him, and if he could find a way to never let me into his courtroom again he would. But he can't do that. Everything I said is true, and attempting to ban me would only make him look worse. So, he's stuck with me, and he now knows that I am more than a match for him!

"Whatever the outcome, Frankie, Longyear now knows that he must be scrupulously fair throughout your trial or the court of public opinion will tear him to pieces."

"So, what happens now?"

"Well, I'm afraid the Top Court will indeed make the change to the law, but I have prevailed on him to delay the proceedings until that's a fact, not just an assumption. In the circumstances, he had no choice but to agree. I assume that will happen by tomorrow and we'll be back in court after the weekend. We won't need theatrics then, just the charge and your 'not guilty' plea. Then a trial date will be set. Any questions?"

I shake my head, and Sinclair jumps up, anxious to get on with preparations. He fastens his briefcase quickly, slips on his jacket and is about to leave, but then hesitates and looks at me kindly.

"Frankie, I think you know this, but I want to be absolutely clear, we are in for a very challenging ride. Zimmerman and his team will attempt to rip your life to pieces, paint you as an uncaring monster who deserves to die. You need to prepare yourself for that onslaught in whatever ways you can. But come what may, no matter what they throw at you, I promise you at every step of the way I will do my utmost to ensure you get a fair trial."

It didn't need saying – Sinclair is so obviously sincere. I want to acknowledge his support and what it means to me.

"Thank you," I say. "That's all I want; a fair trial is all any of us deserve."

Sinclair offers me his hand and I shake it warmly. Then he heads out of the room, and I wait to be taken back to the prison. Excitement flutters in my stomach and I realize that I'm looking forward to this fight!

CHAPTER THIRTY-SEVEN

The guards are respectful on the journey back to the prison and also in the prison itself after I arrive – I assume Sinclair's performance in court sent the message that they need to be more careful how they treat me or there will be consequences. I assume, too, that he let Jess know where to find me because on Saturday afternoon at the visiting hour, I'm taken from my cell to the visitor's room.

It's packed with small groups huddled around Formica-topped tables and smells of perfume and sweat. I scan the room and see Jess, Alex, Shirley and Sylvie waving. It hurts to smile, but I'm thrilled to see them.

A guard chains my left leg to my chair and forbids any physical contact, but the sparkle in Jess's eyes is electric, and I reach across and squeeze her hand.

"It looks worse than it is," I say to defuse the obvious concern written across their faces about my physical appearance. I quickly change the subject. "So, tell me everything! What's been going on?"

Alex leaps straight in. "The broadcast is on every online channel you can imagine, Frankie! And it's the top viewed reel on all of them, from YouTube to Weibo. The whole world knows what went on."

"Weibo?" I ask.

Alex slaps his forehead. "Duh, China of course!" he says in mock frustration. "Where have you been the past few years, living under a rock?"

We all chuckle at his joke, then Jess adds, "You're a global phenomenon, Frankie Green!"

She leans forward to quickly kiss me before a guard tells her to sit back down. We both snigger like kids.

"So, what's the media reaction to yesterday's hearing?" I ask.

They all speak at once, but finally Sylvie's left to explain: "Mixed – split right down the middle on party lines, but the chatter in stores and coffee shops is more uniform. Most love your man Sinclair, and most seem to think that the law change – it's official now, by the way – is not right or fair, that it's just another step on the slippery slope to dictatorship."

It's good to hear and I'm grateful. "Please tell me you guys are not in any trouble for what we did."

"Nothing serious, no; I'm old and inconsequential," Shirley says without hesitation. "My words, no one else's!" she adds when she sees me bridle. "Jess and Sylvie have their journalistic cover. And Alex is too young."

I'm relieved to hear it.

"Actually, since then, everything's been really great, Frankie," Alex says. "I'm now the coolest kid in school! Everyone wants to be friends with the kid whose mom loves the President killer!"

Jess blushes, but we all laugh quietly and quickly, respectful of the somber mood in the room and aware of the dark cloud of my trial on the horizon.

"Yes, and the network is talking big promotions for me and Jess," Sylvie adds.

"And now I'm famous, I'm getting hit on by all the old guys in my community!" Shirley says. But then she quickly changes tack. "But that's not why we're here, Frankie. We want to know how *you're* holding up. This has got to be so tough."

I'm quiet for a moment before I answer. "Thank you. Well, physically, I'm slowly recovering. It's going to take some time, but I'll be fine. Mentally, honestly, I'm strong. Of course, I'm a little scared of what's coming, but where I grew up you knew that if you did wrong you paid the price. And I did wrong, no question, so I'll face whatever comes my way. It's just the right thing to do; I'm ready."

Jess looks like she wants to argue, but the others are quiet. I assume they're thinking about the worst-case scenario I face.

To change the mood, I ask about the state of Shirley's van and what they found when they got back home, whether Black Ops had cleaned up. We chat for another twenty minutes or so about all sorts of things, then the bell goes to signal the end of visiting hour.

They each hug me briefly before they leave, promising to return soon. This time the guards don't intervene.

I feel calm as I turn to head back to my cell and smile when I hear Jess call out, "See you in court!"

CHAPTER THIRTY-EIGHT

The second charging and plea session passes without incident. The galleries are packed again, but there are no more surprises, and when the charge of first-degree murder is laid by Zimmerman, I have no hesitation in confidently pleading "not guilty".

Sinclair follows me back from the courthouse to the prison, where I'm taken under guard to meet him in another anonymous room without windows in the administration block. It's painted gray and the furniture is functional and basic.

Sinclair is pacing when I enter, staring anxiously at the brown-tiled floor and biting his lower lip. But his head snaps up when the guard announces me; he's immediately all business.

"Sit, sit," he says as he pours us both a coffee.

He then slips off his jacket, rolls up his sleeves and seats himself at the head of the table, a yellow notepad in front of him and his Rolex pen poised in his right hand.

"Okay, so, I have some important news for you and then I need to conduct the most thorough interview I've ever conducted, covering everything leading up to and including Teufel's death. Just to prepare you, this will take some time – we are in uncharted waters in many ways now. They didn't think through how the consequences of passing a new law on a whim would ripple out, including on what counts as proof and precisely how the jury will make a decision based on what they hear! But it's too late to worry about that now…" Sinclair smiles grimly. "I must just prepare every angle thoroughly."

I can see his point.

Sinclair continues, "The prison governor has granted me, from tomorrow, four blocks of four hours with you to be used over the next three days. It'll be tight, but if we're efficient we can get through what needs to be done in that time."

"Whatever you need to know, just ask," I say. "But why so tight? What's the rush?"

Sinclair leans back in his seat, undoes his tie, loosens his collar and lets out a long sigh. "Zimmerman demanded that the trial gets underway five days from now, and his buddy the judge granted his request. They argued that the longer we delay the more difficult it will be to empanel an unbiased jury. Unfortunately, they have a point.

"On Monday next week we'll be in court; so, for the next three days, we will prepare. The day before the trial starts, I'll need to enter the various paperwork necessary, so we won't meet that day, but by then you'll know what I want you to work on."

My heart is suddenly pounding. I'm ready to fight, but this is all so unfamiliar and it's happening so fast.

Sinclair notes my concern. He puts down a sheet of questions he has for me, winks and says, "Look, this is going to be high stress, Frankie. There's no doubt about that. But of all the clients I've represented, you are the most prepared to deal with stress. After all, you were trained for combat in the desert so it's really nothing new to you – it's just a different environment, that's all.

"Try not to worry. I actually think Zimmerman might have shot himself in the foot by pushing so hard for an early trial; he really hasn't thought things through very well at all. It's just dawned on him that jury selection will be more complicated because of the publicity surrounding your case, but I don't think he's realized yet just how hard it will be to get the kind of jury he's after. You mark my words."

CHAPTER THIRTY-NINE

The next three days are intense but they pass quickly. By the time we're done, I feel like Sinclair knows everything he needs to know about my life and my time in the service, and that he understands every second of my fateful encounter with President Teufel in the aircraft hangar. He walked me through the CCTV footage from the hangar countless times, pushing me to recall what I was thinking and feeling at every step. His energy and attention to detail were impressive. I'm confident that, whatever the outcome, Sinclair will represent me well.

I'm reflecting on this when the door to my cell suddenly flies open. I'm ordered to stand to attention by a guard I haven't seen before – a wiry-looking, cold-eyed man with a pockmarked face. I'm not due to meet Sinclair, and the guard doesn't respond when I ask where he's taking me.

He moves quickly to cuff my hands behind me, but instead of turning left when we leave the cell, which is the direction I usually take when I meet Sinclair, he puts one hand on my left shoulder, the other in the small of my back, and turns me right. I have no idea what's in this direction, but I recognize the grip – Special Forces basic training. Unusual in a prison guard, but maybe nothing to be concerned about. Even so, I'm now on high alert, conscious of my current limitations; my movements are easier now and my ribs are less painful, but I am still not fully recovered.

I notice that the window in the center of each cell door we pass is locked. They're usually open at this time of the day to give inmates additional air to supplement the single vent in the ceiling and provide a chance for them to chat across the hallway. Actually, there's no sound from inside any of the cells either.

Something is definitely wrong.

I look down and glance quickly left and right to get a glimpse of the guard. His uniform looks as it should – standard prison warden issue: black trousers and tunic with a blue shirt underneath, and a black tie knotted tight at the collar. His shoes give him away though. Combat boots are not prison guard uniform; never have been.

I have a decision to make. If he's Special Forces active service, then he'll be part of a team, and I must act before he reaches the rest of them. But, if I'm wrong and I assault him, and he's just ex-Special Forces now working as a guard and having a bad uniform day, Zimmerman will have further ammunition to use at my trial.

"Where was your last mission?" I ask, keeping my voice calm.

The guard reacts with a short, sharp punch to my kidneys. "Shut the fuck up and keep moving."

I stagger briefly but then regain my footing. "Alright, alright. Calm down," I say. "So, what do you make of the prison governor at this place then?" I add, my tone implying that the governor is someone to be ridiculed.

"He's a fucking idiot," the guard replies, and I know then that he's still active duty – this prison currently does not have a full-time governor, and the last one was a woman.

I step quickly to my left and swing my right foot hard into his groin. But I'm still slow, and he sees it coming; I catch him only a glancing blow.

He immediately bends at the waist and runs at me, hitting me hard in the midriff and tipping me onto my back. Red-hot pain shoots through my ribs. He's fast and sits on top of me, his legs gripping my sides tight, squeezing the breath out of me as he rains blows onto my face.

I can't protect myself with my hands behind my back, but I'm taller than him so my arms and legs are longer levers. I buck and squirm until his leg grip loosens enough for me to arch my back with maximum power and tip him forward over my head.

I swivel and am on one knee when he charges me again. My body is screaming at me to stop, but I ignore the pain and launch myself forward – hard – tucking my chin into my neck as I slam into his mouth. I hear teeth crack and feel blood erupt onto my head, but he won't go down.

As I back away, he moves towards me again. He's swaying slightly but there is fury in his eyes. He wipes the blood away from his mouth, then slips off his prison officer jacket and sets himself to attack.

I hear whistles and the sound of running feet behind me, but I dare not take my eyes off him.

He glances behind me and curses. "You're a lucky bastard!" he snarls, then turns and sprints down the hallway in the direction we'd been walking moments earlier.

A police dog tears past me and bites into his right arm. The dog is hanging off his arm, but he keeps moving, slamming his right shoulder into what turns out to be an unlocked exit to the street. I hear the dog yelp as the door swings shut, then three prison guards charge past me in pursuit.

Two more guards arrive soon after and grip me tightly, one on each arm.

The three guards are back minutes later, the dog following them into the building, limping.

My attacker got away.

CHAPTER FORTY

"How on earth could this have happened?" Sinclair bellows.

The prison's interim management team have joined us in an administration block meeting room to review the event.

"This is a maximum-security prison, and yet someone was able to enter, posing as a staff member, access the cell of the most high-profile prisoner here, make sure they had a guaranteed escape route and ensure that all the cells en route to their chosen exit were completely locked down!"

The acting governor clears his throat to speak.

But Sinclair hasn't finished. "And how did they even know where to find Mr. Green, eh?"

The acting governor's head is down, he looks completely hapless. Despite everything, I feel sorry for him. He clears his throat again and says, "Well there will of course be a full inquiry."

"Inquiry!" Sinclair explodes. "You bet there will be an inquiry, and heads will roll, but it's already plain as day – there is simply no way any of this could have happened without inside help!"

"It's a little early to be saying that, Mr. Sinclair."

Sinclair rises abruptly to his feet, his chair tipping backwards onto the floor, his eyelids fluttering. He sounds incredulous as he stalks around the table spitting words at them.

"Too early to be saying that? So, tell me how it's possible *without* inside help for someone to acquire the uniform of this prison, find out where Mr. Green is being held, make sure that the only door through the two-foot-thick walls of this prison that leads to the street is unlocked, and lock down thirty prisoners' cells so they can see and hear nothing." Sinclair leaves a silence and then slaps his forehead. "Oh, of course, silly me. It's obvious – they must have used magic! Well, thank you for clearing that up, gentlemen."

Sinclair picks up his chair, noisily places it upright and slams himself down into it. The interim prison management team all look down. I glance across at him and he winks at me, his brown eyes sparkling.

I chime in, "Look, I'm certain my attacker was a serving member of the military. And he didn't want me dead – he'd have killed me as soon as he entered my cell if that was his goal. Or, at least, he'd have tried to. The stakes for the government are high in my trial, and the way things have started, I expect they've realized that Mr. Sinclair may have something up his sleeve." I glance across at Sinclair in case he wants to comment, but he's furiously tapping away at his cell phone keypad, so I continue, "I imagine they just wanted to find out if there was more than I've already revealed that could be used at trial to discredit the government. I think that's what this was – they wanted to find out from me what was coming, by whatever means necessary."

Calmly now, Sinclair takes over and addresses the acting governor directly. "Of course, Mr. Green is right. And plainly, he cannot stay here. He must be moved to a different location. Immediately!"

The acting governor makes a note on his cell phone, but then deletes it when Sinclair adds dismissively, "No need to trouble yourself. While Mr. Green was talking, I set the wheels in motion. Now, please leave. Mr. Green and I have some important matters to discuss."

With their heads bowed, the prison team leaves us alone, muttering apologies as they go.

Once he's sure we're alone, Sinclair checks how I'm feeling and, suitably reassured, paces the room. "You'll recall that I said I didn't think Zimmerman had thought things through," he starts, excitedly. "Well, never was that truer than in today's jury selection."

"How so?"

"Let me ask you this, can you think of any case more high-profile than your own?"

"You're asking the wrong man, Sinclair. I've been in the desert for most of the last eight years; I've no idea what kinds of cases have made the news in that time!"

"Of course, of course. Well, let me tell you that there are none. No case has caught the public imagination like yours has. And *everyone* has an opinion. There are many who believe what happened in that hangar was the most appalling crime; others see it as just a terrible accident; and some see it as divine justice, that he got his just desserts.

"So, we've spent the whole day weeding out potential jurors who already have a strong bias one way or the other. Jury selection is not a scientific process, and it's a mistake to draw conclusions from the balance of opinions expressed by potential jurors, but Zimmerman was increasingly rattled by how evenly split opinions seemed to be. At one point, he even pushed the idea that Longyear should dispense with the jury and judge the case himself. Thankfully, Judge Longyear dismissed that suggestion out of hand, but he is utterly frustrated by our inability to form a jury and has insisted that we enter a period of extensive *voir dire*.

I must look blank because Sinclair quickly adds, "Basically, in high profile cases like this, it means a period of much more detailed and wide-ranging questioning to determine if an individual is fair-minded enough to listen to the evidence and follow its trail according to the law, regardless of their starting prejudices."

"Okay…" I say, still not really understanding why he's so excited.

Sinclair flutters his eyelids in irritation again. "It means, my dear man, that it's going to take a lot longer than the prosecution expected to form a jury, and, therefore, we have more time to prepare." A sly smile sneaks across his face. "And there's icing on the cake… Zimmerman is fuming!"

CHAPTER FORTY-ONE

Later that day, I'm moved to a different prison: the Last Door Holding Center. The transport van's windows are again blacked out, and my feet are again shackled. I worry that if the van is attacked my ability to fight will be severely limited, but the two guards accompanying me are young, alert and seem ready to fight if it becomes necessary.

But I needn't have worried, the forty-five minute journey passes without incident.

The Last Door processing area is well lit, clean and modern. The walls are freshly painted off-white and the floors are covered in a hard-wearing blue carpet, which looks new. There is a pervasive smell of vanilla in the air.

"Welcome to the Last Door Holding Center, Mr. Green. I'm officer Hartshorne." The pleasant-looking guard speaks as she emerges from a corner office holding a tablet computer in her right hand. She peppers me with questions about allergies, food preferences and health needs, and taps everything into the tablet. She then leads me down several wide hallways to an open cell door where she stands aside so that I can enter.

"Everything here is remote controlled. The doors lock automatically at 9pm, after dinner, and unlock at 5:30am, for breakfast. Apart from between those times, you are free to move about this wing of the prison as you like.

"There are three other prisoners here presently, all high-profile and violent. They each keep to themselves, but you may see them around, for example in the library or the gym. My advice is not to engage unless they initiate contact. Any questions?"

"Only one," I say. "Do you know when my lawyer, Mr. Sinclair, will be here?"

Officer Hartshorne taps at her hand-held device for a few moments and then says, "He's scheduled for 5pm."

As Hartshorne heads back the way we came, I step into the cell. It's surprisingly large and well lit. The walls are painted a soft shade of blue and the floor is lightly varnished hardwood. There is a separate toilet and shower, and the bed is soft and wide. Opposite the bed, a computer is bolted to a pine-topped desk; a functional, red plastic chair sits in front of it.

I lay down on my back on the bed, link my fingers behind my head and only wake when a young guard knocks to let me know that Sinclair has arrived.

CHAPTER FORTY-TWO

The guard leaves me at the open door of a well-appointed meeting room where Sinclair is waiting for me, a mug of steaming coffee in his right hand. Sinclair shuts the door behind me, and I sink into a high-backed, black leather chair on one side of a long meeting table. Sinclair takes the seat at the head of the table, facing a huge TV monitor on which an agenda is shown.

He waves to a long table to his right, on which sit sandwiches and other snacks, an urn of freshly brewed coffee and an array of soft drinks. "Help yourself to whatever you want whenever you want it, Frankie. We have a lot to get through this evening."

I get myself a glass of water and a banana while Sinclair explains that the jury selection process will conclude by the end of the week. On that basis, the trial will definitely commence the following Monday. It's now Wednesday, so we have limited time left.

Sinclair says, "We've gone over a great deal of background and detail, and I think we're well prepared for whatever Zimmerman might have up his sleeve, but there are still three questions I want to go over with you." He points at the screen and reads out loud. "First, how do you feel about what happened? To be clear, it's not relevant for establishing guilt, but I'm sure Zimmerman will use this line of questioning in the hope of showing an unattractive character flaw."

"But, if it's not relevant, the jury will ignore it, right?" I say.

"Wrong!" Sinclair immediately responds. "A jury's verdict is only ever partially based on the facts. Even though Judge Longyear will instruct them to focus only on the facts, they won't be able to help themselves – we humans are emotional beings and what we think about someone is very often shaped by what we feel about them. Our jurors are just ordinary people selected for an extraordinary job. We must trust that they will do their best, but in the end, if they like you, they will be less inclined to harshness; if they don't like you, the opposite will be true."

I read between the lines of where this is going. "I won't lie, Sinclair. Please don't ask me to do that."

Sinclair nods reassuringly. "I won't," he says. "But there are different ways of telling the truth, and that's what I want to go through, okay?"

I nod, and he moves on to his second question.

"It's a similar theme, going to the question of your character: of all the jobs you could have done in the army, you ended up as a sniper. Why?"

Words immediately jostle in my head, and my mouth opens to speak, but Sinclair holds his hands up to stop me.

"Save it for now, Frankie. We'll discuss it later. Let's get all of the questions out and then dig into each of them in turn, okay?"

"I'm in your hands," I say, "Whatever you think is best."

"So, the last question," Sinclair says. "Why did you run? Surely, an upright, honorable person would have stayed and explained what happened, and cooperated fully with the authorities?"

I nod that I've understood the question and remain quiet, as Sinclair requested.

He quickly adds, "I'm not saying that's my opinion, Frankie, but it's what many people in the country are asking. And Zimmerman will certainly go there."

"No, I get it," I say. "They're all fair questions, and I'm happy to answer them." Especially that last one, I think to myself. That one's easy: I wanted the world to know the truth about Teufel, and if I'd stayed, the truth would never have left that hangar.

CHAPTER FORTY-THREE

The final days before the trial pass quickly. Sinclair is tied up with jury selection but he provides me with homework each day, areas for me to prepare so I'm crystal clear about them if I'm asked. He also gains access to my full military service record and secures the freedom for me to answer questions about what I did, as long as they don't impact national security.

Unfortunately, the right to wear my uniform during the trial is not granted, so Sinclair kindly buys me an off-the-rack charcoal-gray two-piece suit, a white shirt, a red tie and a black version of his slick brogues. He waves away my promises to repay him once I can access my accounts again, but I will anyway. I don't want charity.

I'm calm as I climb into the police van taking me to the courthouse, and the feeling stays with me throughout the journey.

When we arrive, I'm taken to a holding cell beneath the courtroom. Seven polished wood steps lead up from the cell to the dock where I'll be displayed throughout the trial. I can hear the chatter of people entering the court and settling into their seats as the room rapidly fills. Butterflies flutter in my stomach, but

Sinclair has walked me through this experience many times now, so when the time comes, I confidently take the stairs up into the courtroom.

Despite the preparation, my knees feel weak when I reach the top and scan the room. Every green-leather-backed seat is occupied, even on the balcony. The press pack is corralled to the right of the jury, and I spot an artist quickly creating a sketch of me in the dock.

I see Jess in the middle of the second row on the ground floor. She smiles broadly and gives me a thumbs up. I smile back, then stand to attention as Judge Longyear calls the court to order.

When the room is completely quiet, he says, "The privilege of opening the trial for the untimely death of President Teufel carries with it a grave responsibility, unprecedented in modern times. I would like to start by taking the opportunity to thank the members of our jury for respecting our process and putting their normal lives on hold to see that justice is done in this case; it's very much appreciated.

"Let me remind everybody that, with the exception of the cameras used by the networks covering the case, the use of phones or other electronic devices is forbidden in the courtroom. Please turn them off and keep them off."

While Longyear explains how the trial will run, I look across the room at the two rows of men and women who will decide my fate. My jury. Six men and six women across a wide range of ages. Some are well dressed and evidently wealthy, others less so. Almost all of them look both nervous and excited.

They all avoid my gaze except for a tall, elderly man seated second from the end of the second row. He has silver hair in a buzz cut, a goatee beard and a military bearing. His expression is frank, and as he holds my gaze, an appraising look settles on his face. He's impossible for me to read. I keep my countenance respectful, look away and try to tune back in to what Judge Long-year is saying, but the hairs on the back of my neck are raised and I feel the old man's stare long after I've looked away.

"You have been summoned for the case of The People vs. Frank Green, case number 77ER579467. This is a criminal case. The People are represented by the following attorneys. Please stand up as I introduce you so the jury knows who you are: Mr. Zimmerman, Ms. Gorman, Mr. Strong and Mr. De Jonge. The Defendant is represented by his attorney. Please stand up, Mr. Sinclair."

I'm immediately concerned that we're outnumbered. Zimmerman is plainly the lead; Gorman, Strong and De Jonge seem quite junior, but four against one doesn't feel like good odds.

Sinclair seems to have read my mind. He beams at me and winks, then mouths, "Don't worry."

I tune back into Judge Longyear again.

"Frank Green has been charged with the first-degree murder of President Teufel. The fact that he has been charged does not mean he is guilty. Indeed, Mr. Green has pleaded 'not guilty' to the charge raised against him.

"Members of the jury, you must presume that Mr. Green is innocent unless, after considering all of the evidence, you are convinced that the Defendant is guilty beyond reasonable doubt. The Prosecution is seeking the death penalty for Mr. Green. If a majority of the jury finds the Defendant guilty, then that penalty will be carried out."

Sinclair and I have rehearsed this moment; the brutal words spoken aloud don't shock me now, and I remain calm while Judge Longyear spells out the scale of the task facing the jury.

I look again at the individuals who hold my fate in their hands, and this time all of them are looking at me. The jurors seem to be searching my face for signs of innocence or guilt. I'm smartly dressed, but it's got to be hard to see beyond the cuts and bruises inflicted by the police. They are bound to wonder what kind of innocent man carries those marks.

One by one, they look away. All except the elderly man with the military bearing and the buzz cut, who continues to stare at me so intensely that a shiver runs down my spine.

CHAPTER FORTY-FOUR

Zimmerman rises to give his opening remarks. He has a presence about him, an easy athleticism in his movements and a lulling sincerity in his voice. He's dressed in an expensive-looking black suit and a white shirt; his gold cufflinks reflect the court's ceiling lights when he moves. He looks and sounds successful, like somebody whose words you should trust.

"Ladies and gentlemen of the jury, I will demonstrate to you that the defendant killed our beloved President and he..."

I smile to myself as Sinclair jumps up from his seat and yells, "Objection! The opinion polls show clearly that President Teufel was not beloved by all. And Mr. Zimmerman should not attempt to bias the jury by revealing his own preferences."

"Overruled," Judge Longyear says.

Sinclair gives him a long look and sits down slowly.

Unruffled, Zimmerman continues, "I will demonstrate that not only did the defendant, Frank Green" – Zimmerman jabs his finger at me as he says my name – "kill the President callously in cold blood, but that he did so because that's simply what he's built to do. You see, in one way, he just can't help it; maybe we should even feel sorry for him. After all, he's a natural born killer, and our government recognized that fact and exploited his talents to the full. Killing was his job! And when he was sent abroad to kill, he escaped once the job was done; yes, just like he did when he killed our President then ran from the scene, rather than staying to face the consequences. And to rub salt into the wounds of a grieving nation…"

Sinclair has trained me not to react, but it's hard. Zimmerman's characterization is grossly unfair. I struggle to control my reactions, relax and allow Sinclair to do that job for me.

He is on his feet again, irritation and contempt mingled in his voice, "Objection! Another attempt to manipulate."

"Overruled," Longyear repeats.

Sinclair again gives the judge a long look, then looks across at me, a puzzled expression on his face. He hurriedly writes a few lines on his notepad, then puts his pen down, sits back in his chair, folds his arms across his chest and stares at the judge, hard.

Zimmerman pauses for a moment, slightly distracted by Sinclair's behavior, but then picks up his theme again. "Mr. Green systematically lied to the gullible people he met while he was on the run. The web of lies he wove tied them into actions they would never ordinarily have taken, pushing them to create a broadcast which contained lie after lie, defaming President Teufel, all to create a smoke screen to hide behind.

"Well, no more, ladies and gentlemen of the jury. We will shine the harsh light of truth on Green and show that he is guilty of first-degree murder, and that he deserves to die!"

I want to grab Zimmerman by the throat and punch him until he cries like a baby, but Sinclair has coached me well. I remain outwardly calm and simply shake my head. But I can see that Jess is seething.

Unable to contain herself, she jumps out of her seat and advances towards Zimmerman, yelling, "Liar, liar!"

Guards grab her arms and drag her, kicking and screaming, from the courtroom. I jump up, but Sinclair waves his hands at me in a steadying motion, and I sit down again.

Quick on his feet, Zimmerman uses the moment to add a flourish to his opening statement. "You see, ladies and gentlemen, the Svengali in the dock still exerts his power. That young lady is the one he lured into making that preposterous broadcast, and then he lured her into his bed!"

There are gasps from the public gallery. The jury reacts, too, chattering to each other; stern glances come my way as they do so. The silver-haired man with the buzz cut remains aloof and leans forward in his seat, staring at me intently, his dark eyes shining. I hold his gaze, and he settles back into his seat and looks down. After a moment, he nods to himself as if he's found the answer to a question that's been puzzling him.

Longyear announces a thirty-minute break. "When we return, Mr. Sinclair will deliver his opening remarks."

CHAPTER FORTY-FIVE

During the break, as we take refreshments from the aluminum-framed drinks cart placed in the corner of the holding room under the court, Sinclair counsels me again about the need to project a calm face in court. But as we sit down at the table, he changes the direction of our conversation, his voice measured and soft as if he doesn't want us to be overheard. I lean forward.

"Something very wrong is happening, Frankie. The objections I made were legitimate, but Longyear dismissed them out of hand. I told you he's ambitious and probably wants to make a statement with this case... well, I think we're starting to see that my fears were well founded. I'll be watching how he handles things over the next couple of sessions, but just so you are prepared, I intend to needle him and Zimmerman in my opening remarks, just to see how they react." Sinclair is clearly relishing the prospect.

"What about Jess?" I ask. "After what happened, can she still be called as a witness?"

"Oh yes, if she's up for it, she absolutely can," Sinclair says. "And she really should. Let's be clear, Zimmerman bullied her out there and attacked her in the most cowardly way! Jess deserves the chance to represent herself properly."

I nod, pleased that she will get her chance to fight back. We sit in silence while Sinclair turns something over in his mind.

My thoughts drift to the old guy on the jury, and I break the silence. "Tell me about the juror sitting second from the left on the second row. He looks like a former military guy, silver hair, goatee beard. You know the one?"

"Oh yes, one of Zimmerman's picks," Sinclair says. "He is indeed former military. Reached the rank of colonel in the Intelligence Corps, Colonel James Allen. A card-carrying member of Teufel's party since he was sixteen years old. Why do you ask?"

I explain what I felt in the courtroom, and Sinclair listens carefully.

"Interesting," he says. "He made me uneasy when we were selecting the jury, but his record is impeccable, and I could find no reason to remove him. He claimed to be open to the evidence, but the fact that he's been on Teufel's side of the fence all his adult life still worries me. I can certainly see why Zimmerman put him forward – as a senior military officer, his natural disposition is likely to be in favor of following the rules."

"So, just a senior officer with a natural antipathy to soldiers stepping out of line?" I say.

Sinclair nods, but I feel like we're missing something.

CHAPTER FORTY-SIX

If Zimmerman projected elegance and success with his immaculate clothes, confidence and languid delivery, as Sinclair readies himself for his opening remarks, he projects the image of a bullish street fighter. He takes off his expensive jacket and places it on the back of his chair; he adjusts his red braces and rolls up his sleeves, revealing muscular forearms; then he moves quickly towards the jury, making two elderly women in the front row flinch. I glance at the old colonel, who is suppressing a smile, evidently enjoying the moment.

"Ladies and gentlemen, Mr. Zimmerman has already distorted several basic facts of this case and attempted to manipulate you. I'm not sure why the judge allowed that to go unchallenged, but please be alert for similar distortions as the trial unfolds."

"Objection," Zimmerman says lazily, not stirring from the high-backed seat on which he sits comfortably cross-legged. "Defamation of opposing counsel, Your Honor."

"Objection sustained," Longyear says.

Sinclair looks at the jury and spreads his arms, his expression pure bafflement. Then he shakes his head in resignation and paces slowly backwards and forwards in front of the jury. Their heads turn to follow him as he talks, his voice modulated and soothing.

"The person Mr. Zimmerman has described is not the man who sits in the dock today. I will show you that Frank Green is in fact a hero, a man who lived his life in the shadows with no public recognition but who has played a vital role in keeping us all safe, a man of integrity who has served this country well and done so with pride." He stops pacing and raises his voice. "Pride that President Teufel crushed by turning him into his own personal assassin." He smashes his right fist into his hand for emphasis. "When Frankie Green learned, much too late to change things, that he'd been used, it was simply too much for him.

"There is no doubt that he reacted badly. But I ask you, who wouldn't react badly when they find out they have been betrayed, turned into an unwitting murderer instead of a legitimate operative working to keep his country safe?"

I scan the jury; several are nodding in agreement, others are stone faced. The former colonel is staring at me, not at Sinclair, his face impassive. I feel another shiver run down my spine.

I refocus on Sinclair as he picks up speed. "I will show you that President Teufel's death was not planned by Mr. Green, not at all. I will show you that this is a case of a corrupt state that will stop at nothing in pursuit of its own selfish goals – so ruthless that they intend to use you, too. They will use you to put to death one of our country's heroes: Captain Frank Green!"

Sinclair has silenced the courtroom. Except for the old colonel, the jury is in the palm of his hand. He nods briefly and respectfully to the jury, then turns away to retake his seat.

Zimmerman claps slowly, a bored expression on his face. I want to punch him but keep my expression neutral.

Sinclair stops mid-stride, his fists momentarily balled and the muscles in his arms bulging. He spins abruptly back to face the jury.

"Oh, I almost forgot. You are, of course, all aware of how, at Mr. Zimmerman's request, our Top Court changed the law to allow the charge of first-degree murder to be laid on Mr. Green's shoulders. Well, there is one consequence of that ill-considered action and the rush to use it that has not yet been spelled out for you, and I really should make it clear now." Sinclair glances across at Zimmerman, who is now leaning forward in his seat, finally curious to hear what Sinclair has to say. Sinclair suppress a smile and again paces as he speaks. "Judge Longyear has explained that if you find Mr. Green guilty of first-degree murder then you must also sentence him to death." Sinclair stops and looks up expectantly at the jury, waiting for a response. After a moment or two everyone nods, including the colonel. "Those of you who were listening carefully will have noticed that first-degree murder is the *only* charge laid, right?"

I wonder where he's going with this line of argument and lean forward as he waits for the jury to acknowledge the fact. When they do, he steps up to the rail in front of the first row and places both of his hands on it.

His voice rises slightly as he speaks, very deliberately. "Mr. Zimmerman is a very confident man. He is confident that enough of you will follow his direction and end Mr. Green's life – all he needs is a simple majority. Indeed, so confident is he of that result that he didn't consider it necessary to bring additional charges.

"I am not so arrogant. I know that I need to earn your trust, I need to convince you of a very different explanation for the facts of this case. But if I do so, you must acquit my client. *There is no lesser charge that you may consider.*"

I'm stunned and, judging by their expressions, so too are the jury.

Zimmerman jumps up in outrage. "Utter nonsense. Judge Longyear, please direct the jury correctly!"

Longyear sits back in his chair heavily and strokes his chin, lost in thought for a full minute. Sinclair looks up at me and winks.

When Longyear finally speaks, his voice falters slightly. "Mr. Zimmerman, Mr. Sinclair, join me at my bench, please."

The two lawyers do as they are asked, and the three men huddle together in conclave. I can hear their raised voices, but I cannot make out what they are saying.

The conversation is short. Zimmerman curses Longyear under his breath as he returns to his seat, and Sinclair looks serious as he walks over to the jury. He thanks them for their attention and then returns to his seat, too.

Then Longyear speaks. "Ladies and gentlemen of the jury, you may know that since President Teufel's re-election, many adjustments to statute have been made. As a result of those changes, what Mr. Sinclair told you is correct. The charge of first-degree murder is now either up or down; yes, the charge of first-degree murder has been proven or no, it has not. So, if you do *not* find Mr. Green guilty of President Teufel's murder in the first degree, then, as Mr. Sinclair has stated, you must set him free."

Sinclair hadn't explained this to me. I sit back in my seat, astonished at the news and wondering why he didn't brief me before we went back into court. A cacophony fills the courtroom. Sinclair looks up at me and winks again.

I watch the jury carefully as they fervently chat to each other, all except the colonel, who is staring at the floor in front of him.

After a couple of minutes, the jury quietens down and the foreman hands the court runner a note for the judge. Longyear reads the note, folds it and places it in the folder on the table in front of him. Then he leans into his microphone.

"The jury has asked for direction. They've asked what to do if they find the defendant not guilty of the first-degree murder of President Teufel, but they believe he did cause the President's death. Can they ask for his conviction on a lesser charge, such as manslaughter?" Judge Longyear takes a breath before continuing, regret dripping from his words, "For complete clarity, ladies and gentlemen of the jury, I have to tell you that the option to convict on a lesser charge is *not* available to you – even if you believe that Mr. Green is responsible for President Teufel's death but that he did not commit murder in the first degree. The charges brought by Mr. Zimmerman were singular not multiple. I repeat, Mr. Sinclair is correct, you either convict Mr. Green of first-degree murder or you set him free."

I'm bewildered. It doesn't seem right. I killed the President. Whether it was directly or indirectly doesn't matter; the fact remains that if it wasn't for me, he'd still be alive! I glance across at the jury and see angry eyes, mouths wide open, stunned faces staring at the judge as if they cannot believe their ears. Only the colonel is calm. He's sitting upright with his hands on his knees looking down at the floor, deep in thought.

Longyear, suddenly looking exhausted, says, "Court is adjourned for a one-hour recess."

The members of the jury are quickly on their feet, chattering feverishly as they leave. Except, again, the colonel, who remains seated, staring at the floor.

Then, he lifts his head and looks directly at me. And for the first time, a brief smile cracks his face.

CHAPTER FORTY-SEVEN

I return to the holding area, and when Sinclair joins me, I immediately lean into him and demand answers. "Why didn't you tell me beforehand?"

He doesn't respond immediately, just helps himself to a cup of coffee and bites into a bright red apple, taken from the bowl of fresh fruit on the side table and polished vigorously on his trouser leg. He smiles coyly and blushes slightly. "Yes, sorry about that. A bit of court drama can be very useful.

"I wanted the jury to see your reaction to the news, so you had to hear it when they did. I had the feeling that you'd be as shocked as they were and look just as outraged, and indeed that's exactly what happened. You really did look outraged that the jury couldn't convict you of at least some crime, even if they didn't believe you committed first-degree murder! The fact that every other person alive would have jumped for joy in that situation won't have been lost on them. Remember, actions speak louder than words; I told the jury that you are an upstanding man of fine character, and now they've seen a glimpse of that man for themselves."

I realize there's a lot more to Sinclair than meets the eye, and I'm starting to believe that I couldn't be in better hands.

***

Zimmerman is animatedly talking to Longyear when we return to the courtroom, and while the jury retake their positions, Longyear beckons Sinclair to join them.

I watch closely and try to read their body language. Shortly after joining them, Sinclair shakes his head vigorously, but the judge's demeanor suggests that he's made up his mind.

Sinclair turns and walks slowly back to his seat. As he passes, he looks up at me and shakes his head in frustration.

I don't have to wait long to learn why. Judge Longyear bangs his gavel, calling the court to order. "Mr. Zimmerman has asked the court to grant a deviation from protocol. He has asked for a new witness to be called – one not originally scheduled. This is unusual; normally, each side in a case is obliged to provide a list of the witnesses they will call during the course of a trial so that each side can prepare, but the particular witness Mr. Zimmerman wants to call is in a position of extreme responsibility, and because of these responsibilities, Mr. Zimmerman did not believe it would be possible for this witness to attend. As a result, he was not on the list provided to Mr. Sinclair. However, the witness has suddenly become available, and given his relevance to the case, I have allowed an exception.

"However, we must prepare the courtroom, so, with apologies, we will go back into recess for a further thirty minutes to allow the necessary adjustments to be made."

∗∗∗

Sinclair walks straight to the conference table in the holding area, rests his bodyweight on his balled-up fists and stares at the coffee stains that pattern the table's surface. After a few moments, he whips his head up and stands straight, his eyes molten with anger and a grim, determined look on his face.

I lean forward expectantly.

"Frankie, prepare yourself. When we go back into the courtroom, Zimmerman will call the VP, or, should I say, Acting President."

I'm startled into silence.

"In all my years of practicing law, I've never come across anything as outrageous as this. Longyear should never have allowed it, it's a complete breach of protocol." Sinclair's voice rises in frustration. "We have no time to prepare cross-examination questions – I'll just have to wing it!" He draws breath then starts to pace again, head down in thought.

Finally, he comes to a stop, and when he speaks his voice is calmer. "The thing is, Frankie, I think Zimmerman has had this set up for a while and just didn't tell us. He's blindsided us."

"How so?" I ask.

"Well, for a start, Zimmerman was calm when he made his request to the judge, and Longyear was not nearly as surprised as he would have been if it was genuinely a surprise. They should be scrambling like I am; their calmness tells its own story. We'll know for certain when the proceedings start – if things go smoothly, then we'll know for sure that Zimmerman knew this was coming and deliberately kept us in the dark."

Sinclair is fighting hard for me, but it suddenly feels like the walls are closing in. Like no matter what Sinclair does, the prosecution will twist and turn to get the conviction they desperately want and Longyear's career needs. My heart pounds and I'm suddenly bathed in a layer of sweat.

Sinclair instantly recognizes my concern. "Look, Frankie, there is no doubt that since President Teufel's re-election the law has been under siege – the courts have been flooded with Teufel loyalist judges and new legislation has been forced through for no reason other than to suit Teufel's needs. Don't forget, he faced multiple legal issues before his re-election and he needed them to go away in a hurry. But Frankie, rushing legislation is never a good idea; look closely enough and there's usually a flaw to be found. I need to start digging deeper."

He smiles but I can't shake the feeling that all we're doing is delaying the inevitable. But a glimmer of hope comes to mind. "But at least you'll be able to question the VP, right? Expose his lies?"

Sinclair nods. "That's right, Frankie. Now, if you'll excuse me, I need to quickly draft a few questions before we're called back."

I leave Sinclair at the table scribbling furiously, help myself to a glass of water and sit quietly in the corner of the holding room. I focus on my breathing and slow my heartrate down – an essential sniper drill I've practiced thousands of times. My head clears, then the sound of the judge's gavel banging draws us back into the court.

CHAPTER FORTY-EIGHT

In the brief period we've been away, a large, electrically operated screen has been lowered from the ceiling to the left of the judge; a projector mounted beneath the balcony is projecting a powerful beam onto it.

As I settle back onto my wooden stool, I look across at the jury. Their attention is on Zimmerman, who has stepped away from his desk to stand in the center of the room. He cuts a commanding figure.

With a slightly theatrical flourish, he loudly says, "I call the Acting President to the stand."

Subdued chatter engulfs the courtroom. Longyear bangs his gavel several times to regain order.

The former Vice President strolls confidently to the front of the court, flanked by two heavily built bodyguards. Two more guards stand at the court's rear, by the entrance doors. The former VP is trim in an expensive-looking, dark suit. His thick hair is slicked back off his high forehead, a physical characteristic he inherited from his mother. His facial features are delicate, and a slightly receding chin carries a neatly trimmed beard.

Zimmerman swears him in, makes sure a request for a glass of water is attended to, and then begins, his voice syrupy and fawning. "Mr. Acting President, the court cannot thank you enough for making time for this."

"Wild horses couldn't keep me away," the Acting President says, his voice strong and loud. Then he points directly at me and shouts at the jury, "I came because I want to see that son of a bitch fry for killing my dad!" Then, abruptly, the Acting President puts his left hand on his brow and covers his eyes, and his body shakes as if he's crying.

Zimmerman calls to the court runner urgently, "Tissues, please."

The Acting President dabs his eyes and quickly regains his composure – a little too quickly in my opinion. I glance at the jury, hoping to see skepticism on their faces, but instead I see one or two dabbing tissues at the corners of their own eyes and the rest looking concerned for him – except for the colonel, whose expression remains neutral.

Zimmerman picks up a small remote-control device. "When you're ready, I'd like to run through the CCTV of the meeting between you and the accused in the hangar, which preceded that fateful meeting between your father and the accused. Are you okay with that?"

A ripple of chatter swells around the court but is over quickly. Sinclair looks furious.

The Acting President confirms that he's happy to do as he's been asked.

"Thank you!" Zimmerman says. "So, as the video runs, I'm going to ask you a few questions, okay?"

The Acting President nods, and Zimmerman starts the CCTV recording. The camera must have been above the hangar door, and it takes in the whole space. The black and white film is grainy and there's no sound, but it's clear enough.

On the screen we see the then VP standing alone on a raised platform, then I come into view, fresh off the plane and ragged-looking. I remember the moment clearly, just minutes before my life changed completely.

"Please tell us in your own words what's happening here," Zimmerman says.

The Acting President sits up straight in his chair and tugs at his elegant, tailored jacket to straighten it across his shoulders. He then addresses the jury, his voice dripping with sincerity.

"Well, as you can see, Green has just come into the hangar and come directly over to me, belligerently, demanding to see the President."

I'm dumbfounded. That's not what happened, and not a conclusion that anyone could legitimately draw from the images on the screen. I lean forward to get Sinclair's attention, but he just nods at me to stay calm and makes some notes that I assume he'll use in his cross-examination of the Acting President.

Several jury members stare at me, their faces angry and accusing. It's unsettling, but I try to ignore it and focus on what the Acting President is saying. When I do, I'm outraged – he is inventing a completely false account, taking advantage of the lack of sound and the fact that my face cannot be seen because the camera is behind me.

"Green was furious that the President wasn't there to greet him, seemed to think he deserved that honor!"

Zimmerman interjects when the video reaches the point that I tell the then VP that the kill has been performed, and the VP ticks off the final name on the paper he was holding. "At this point, you appear to ask Green a question and make a note of his response. Is that right?"

"Well, yes and no. I simply asked him how he was and explained that the President would be along as soon as he could. The piece of paper is something else entirely. I asked him how he was feeling, and when he grunted a reply, I just carried on working through a list of candidates for a secretarial post I was hiring for. So, the paper I'm holding is completely unrelated to my brief exchange with Green."

I can barely sit still as most of the jury nod their understanding. The Acting President is so calm, confident and believable, but every word is a lie. I feel screams welling up inside me. I push the feeling down, but I can't sit still. I leap forward and lean over the edge of the box towards Sinclair and hold my hands out wide to convey my frustration. I mouth, "He's lying!" Sinclair again acknowledges me but stays silent.

Zimmerman stands next to the Acting President, his eyes on the jury. "In his broadcast, Mr. Green showed the world a list of names written on Presidential note paper. Each name had been ticked off. He claimed that the last name was his final kill and that all of the people listed had been killed because they objected to President Teufel's plans for a golf course in their country. And he claimed that he picked it up off the floor when you dropped it as you left to take over from the President. What do you make of that?"

The Acting President turns his attention to me and holds my gaze as he says, "Lies, all of it. Despicable lies. I took the piece of paper he saw me scribbling on with me, and in any case, my father never tried to get a golf course built in that god-forsaken country, ever. But if he had, by God he would have succeeded. He was a winner in everything. His loss has robbed this country of its greatest ever leader!" Then the Acting President points at me and says, "HE robbed us of our greatest ever leader!" Then he's on his feet in front of the jury, still pointing at me and yelling, "For that, this man deserves to die! Frank Green is guilty! Do your jobs and make him pay!"

The courtroom erupts. Several jurors stand and clap the Acting President's speech, harsh judgment stamped on their faces. The colonel remains seated and is again watching me closely.

My outrage has become cold anger. My mind is clear; everything seems to have slowed down a fraction, allowing me to take in every detail. From my vantage point, I can see the entire court. The jury's furious reaction is mirrored across the room. But then my attention is drawn to one of the Acting President's guards by the doors at the entrance to the courtroom; he's leaning into the door, but his phone is clearly visible and he's tapping at the keypad like he's making a call!

Zimmerman sits down again and receives congratulatory pats on the shoulder from his team. Sinclair is immediately on his feet, ready to cross-examine the Acting President – then a phone rings. Longyear says nothing, despite his opening statement forbidding phone use during the trial. The ringing sound continues. Then the Acting President takes his phone from his inside jacket pocket and answers the call. I watch the guard at the door immediately put away his phone without saying a word.

The Acting President appears to listen intently and, thirty seconds later, puts his phone back in his inside pocket, stands and addresses Judge Longyear, "Sir, I am so sorry, but I need to leave immediately. Matters of national security – I'm sure you understand." He reaches up and shakes the judge's hand.

"Of course, Mr. Acting President. No problem," Longyear replies warmly.

I'm on my feet, trying to attract Sinclair's attention, but he doesn't see me. He's already moving to block the Acting President's path to the door.

When the Acting President is forced to stop, Sinclair politely but firmly says, "Sir, I have several important questions for you, and our system of justice provides the opportunity for cross-examination. Please retake your seat."

The Acting President looks completely unconcerned and says dismissively, "Yes, no doubt, but I need to leave right now. I'll leave you to sort that issue out with the judge." With that, he steps around Sinclair and strides towards the door.

Sinclair is blocked from following by one of the Acting President's security detail. I watch him try to push past, but the security guy is clearly experienced – there's no way Sinclair will slip by him.

Then the Acting President stops as he passes the jury. "Ladies and gentlemen, you know what needs to be done. Honor the memory of my father and convict that man." He turns to point at me again.

The court is in uproar. My mind and body react as I've trained them to do in high-danger situations when becoming too emotional could get me killed – my heartrate slows, my blood pressure drops and my mind slows down, enabling me to see all the details I need.

One by one, I calmly scan the jury's faces, keeping my own expression neutral. Several look away and won't engage with me, but I count five whose faces are like granite – hard and unforgiving.

I come to the colonel last, aware that he's been watching me the whole time. He's leaning forward, his hands under his chin, supporting his head. When I make eye contact, his expression remains neutral, like mine – an old soldier, calm in the gathering storm. He looks at the witness stand and then back at me. He does it twice. He's sending me a message – testify, now!

I sit back and take in the whole scene. Sinclair is angrily re-monstrating with the judge, Zimmerman appears to be arguing back, and the rest of the courtroom is in pandemonium. Long-year has lost control.

Eventually, he bangs his gavel and calls a recess. I run down the steps to the holding room and wait for Sinclair to arrive.

CHAPTER FORTY-NINE

Sinclair bursts into the room a few minutes later, deep in thought. He silently pours us both coffee, and I wait. He sits at the head of the table and has finished his coffee when he's finally ready to speak.

"Frankie, today we witnessed yet more evidence that our justice system is under siege. It strains all credibility that Zimmerman just happened to have the CCTV footage available and that a nice line of questioning just came to his mind. But that's what they claim. Yes, I did say 'they.' Judge Longyear is plainly in on it. And it's beyond the pale that the Acting President could waltz in, deliver the messages he wanted to deliver and then waltz out again with no cross-examination. It's unheard of! Like so many things since Teufel's second term began!

"I have at least forced Longyear to instruct the jury to ignore what the Acting President said because we did not get the right of reply. No one can unhear what's been said though, especially when it was said so compellingly. And you have to give the Acting President credit for that – he's a great actor!"

Sinclair is quiet for a moment, lost in thought again, and then says, "I'm sorry to say but I'm afraid Zimmerman's shenanigans have torn our defense strategy to shreds. Things are not unfolding at all as we planned. We need to think again."

I've reached the same conclusion, so I nod, and we both sit. I then unhurriedly share what I noticed in the lead-up to the Acting President's phone call. I also share what I observed of the jury's reaction to the Acting President's demands, including the colonel's.

Sinclair looks thoughtful and we both sit silent for a moment. Then we speak simultaneously, our words colliding:

"I want to take the stand!"

"It's time they find out who you really are!"

We quickly go over Zimmerman's ideas for the session and the key themes that we think the jury should hear.

There are butterflies in my stomach as I take the steps back up to the courtroom, but I'm ready – ready to fight for my life.

CHAPTER FIFTY

Before Sinclair calls me to the stand, Judge Longyear instructs the jury to dismiss what they heard from the Acting President. But it's clear from his tone that his heart's not in it, and it's clear from the jury's expressions that they will ignore his instruction.

While Longyear delivers his opening remarks, Sinclair, as planned, signals to the court runner, hands him a sheet of folded paper and whispers something in his ear. The runner glances at the paper, refolds it and heads out of the court through the judge's chamber.

As soon as the judge is finished speaking, Sinclair calls me to the stand.

Zimmerman is on his feet immediately. "Objection! This is a change in the running order that we were not advised of."

I pass the judge on my way to the stand, and it's clear from his face that he's looking for a way to support Zimmerman's objection but is struggling to do so given his ready accommodation of the Acting President. Sinclair glares at the judge, daring him to deny me the opportunity to speak.

After a long pause, Longyear overrules Zimmerman's objection.

The courtroom is daunting from the witness stand – banks of TV cameras are trained on me, the jury is staring at me hard and, right in front of me, the press and public galleries are full to overflowing. Then I spot Jess, Alex, Sylvie and Shirley waving from the back of the public gallery balcony. I feel centered again and ready.

Sinclair starts, gently at first, with a question about my childhood. "Mr. Green, please share with the jury what you recall about the place you grew up."

"Oakvale was my whole world as a kid," I start. "A busy little hard-working town, where everyone knew everyone." I can hear the sincere enthusiasm in my voice as I recall those days. "Everyone did their best to take care of their own family, but if someone fell on hard times, you know, like they fell ill or lost their job or couldn't afford the doctor, we all helped out as best we could. There was no obligation to do that and no expectation that we'd be repaid, it was just the right thing to do. It was what we'd always done in Oakvale since the first settlers, before health insurance and such."

"Thank you," Sinclair says. "And did you always want to join the army?"

I can feel the jury's eyes boring into me. "No, not at all. I wanted to be a doctor. In fact, I'm sure I would have become a doctor if the mill hadn't failed – my grades were good enough – but when money got tight I needed to find work, to help Mom and Dad keep a roof over our heads. There was just no work to be had locally, so I joined up like most of my buddies, it was kind of a needs-must thing."

"Oh," Sinclair says, feigning surprise. "But I thought Mr. Zimmerman said you were a natural born killer?"

I'm expecting Zimmerman to object, but he remains in his seat. He and his team are watching the jury's reactions closely, and so far, their faces are impassive.

I stand up straight as I answer the question, "Mr. Zimmerman did indeed say that, but nothing could be further from the truth. Circumstances took me into the army, and the army chose to use my skills as they saw fit. I did not choose to be a sniper and I could not force the army to deploy me differently. That's not how it works."

The colonel nods in agreement. The jurors around him notice but their faces remain neutral.

Then, the tone of questioning shifts.

"So, how does it feel to kill someone, Mr. Green? To take a life?"

It feels as though the entire court draws in a breath. We planned for this, and I knew it was coming, but I struggled with this question during our preparations and I'm still not comfortable – raw emotion churns through my stomach whenever I think about what I've done.

"It's sickening," I say. "Every person I killed for our government has left a mark on my soul, and the passage of time doesn't make it any easier. Each of them had a family. It's no matter that someone is our country's enemy; no one is all bad and neither are their families. But my actions left families grieving, and grief never really goes away, you just learn to carry it better as time goes by."

I take a sip of water and notice Zimmerman scribbling on a notepad. I glance at the jury. Several are nodding; I assume it's because they recognize their own moments of grief in what I've said. One says quietly, "So true."

"Do you resent the government for making you do what you did?"

"Not at all," I answer immediately. "It was my job. It was my duty. I didn't question it."

Sinclair paces in front of the jury, nodding. Following his lead, several jurors nod too.

We skirt around the details of several missions, keeping secure those aspects that could compromise the government. I'm happy that that the stories shared give an accurate representation of the work I did.

Then, as planned, Sinclair addresses the judge. "Your Honor, I'd like to run the CCTV tape again. The one that Mr. Zimmerman used with the Acting President."

As expected, Zimmerman objects, and Sinclair, Zimmerman and Longyear enter into a heated debate at the judge's bench.

Finally, glowering, Zimmerman returns to his seat, and Longyear orders the tape to be run.

Sinclair steps close to me as preparations are made to run the footage and says, "I have an idea, trust me," he says.

I have no idea what he has in mind, but I trust his judgment so I nod my support. I notice the jury are all leaning forward expectantly.

As the film starts, Sinclair says, "Okay, Mr. Green. Please do what the Acting President did earlier and share with us at each step what you recall from this exchange."

Watching the grainy footage of the then-VP in the hangar on his own, I say, "Well, you can't see me in the picture, but at this point I've just stepped down from the mission plane and been told that the President wants to see me in the hangar."

"Was that normal?" Sinclair says.

"Not at all. I've met several presidents, at award ceremonies and such, but never straight after returning from operational duties." I am now visible on the screen, walking into the hangar and across to the then-VP.

"The Acting President says you were belligerent when you spoke to him."

I look across at the jury. I want them to see my face clearly when I say, as calmly as I can, "He's lying. In fact, everything he said about this exchange was untrue." Several jurors look shocked by my bluntness, but I continue, the conviction growing in my voice. "Look, when I landed, I had no idea the President was at the base. And when I spoke to the VP, I didn't know why this particular mission was so important to the President. The only exchange the VP and I had was about the mission. He asked me one question: Was my target dead?"

"Ok," Sinclair continues, "now let's keep the tape running and, as we do so, please continue to share your memories of what's shown, Mr. Green."

Zimmerman is again on his feet. "No, absolutely not. We will not share with the world the moment our beloved President died!"

Arguments for and against showing the CCTV footage ripple through the gallery, then Judge Longyear bangs his gavel in frustration and declares an adjournment, demanding that Sinclair and Zimmerman join him in his chambers.

Sinclair is the last of the three to leave the courtroom. As he reaches the door to the judge's chambers, I spot the runner return and signal Sinclair to wait for him. Sinclair smiles and gives me a thumbs-up as he waits. But his expression changes as the runner speaks to him, and as he pushes the judge's door open, his face is full of fury.

I hurry to the holding room and force myself to be patient, hoping Sinclair will join me before the session reconvenes.

When he doesn't, a knot of anxiety takes root in my stomach.

CHAPTER FIFTY-ONE

Sinclair is still in the judge's rooms when I take my seat in the dock, but he reappears soon after, frowning. He gives me a brief wave before taking his seat, then immediately sets to work reviewing his stack of handwritten notes. I glance across to Zimmerman's team, who have gathered into a circle. They're chatting animatedly and exchanging high fives.

Longyear leans into his microphone and addresses the court, "Ladies and gentlemen, the opposing councils have each made their case" – as I listen as the knot in my stomach grows – "but I am still undecided on how to proceed with respect to showing the next sections of the CCTV recording, particularly given their sensitive nature. I am going to take the evening to reflect on the matter. Court is adjourned for the day. Proceedings will recommence at eight am tomorrow."

Longyear quickly heads back to his chambers, and the court empties quickly. When I am ready to take the steps to my holding area, almost everyone has gone. Sinclair is still seated, though, lost in thought. I call down to him, stirring him from his reverie. He quickly jumps up and gathers his things.

He's still preoccupied when he enters the holding room and flops into a seat at the table. I pour him a glass of water then sit down too.

After a couple of minutes, he clears his throat and says in a firm voice, "Frankie, I want to apologize. I did not expect this to be an easy ride but I also did not expect the State to try and undermine us at every turn – but that is exactly what's happening. They've derailed the normal process at every turn! The nonsense with the Vice President was serious enough, but attempting to prevent video evidence being shown of the very events in question is unforgivable. Utterly unprofessional!

"And even worse, just before I entered the judge's chambers, I learned that the list you showed in your broadcast, the list of golf club development opponents you were ordered to kill, is missing. And it's the *only* piece of evidence missing, which can only mean that it was targeted for removal."

I'm stunned. "So, what now?" I say, the knot in my stomach evolving into a sense of dread.

Sinclair replies, "Look, Frankie, I have something in mind, but it's new and I need to check that I have my facts straight. If I do then, when we reconvene tomorrow, I will come out with all guns blazing and give them a taste of their own medicine. So, if you'll excuse me, I have a long night ahead of me. I'll see you here bright and early in the morning, though, and until then, try to get some rest. Easier said than done, I know, but please try."

As I move to wait by the door for the guard to take me back to the prison, Sinclair adds, "Oh, meant to tell you, I'm seeing Jess later, she wanted to hear first-hand where we're at. I'll give her your love."

I didn't know Jess and Sinclair were in touch, but I'm pleased to hear it.

On the way back to the prison, however, as the guards sit in silence and we rock from side to side with the road's undulations, the stark reality of my situation stares me in the face like the barrel of a gun. The State has seen to it that our plans are in tatters, and my fate now rests on whatever final play Sinclair conjures up in the next few hours.

It's all so ragged and ad hoc, a perversion of what our founders intended. Sadly, it's our new reality since Teufel set about dismantling the apparatus of our democracy.

CHAPTER FIFTY-TWO

The next morning, on the way to the courthouse, the guards are animated as they discuss something from the news. I try to listen in but catch only snippets that make no sense. They seem to be looking differently at me, too, but perhaps I'm imagining it.

The same excited energy is in the air as I pass through the courthouse to the holding cell, and when I enter the cell, Sinclair is already at the worktable, smiling broadly.

"Morning, Frankie," he says more brightly than the heavy bags under his eyes suggest he has a right to. "Sleep well?"

I laugh. "As well as you'd expect! I wish I felt as cheery as everyone else seems to be today, though."

"I hear you, Frankie, but please take a seat. I think I have something to lift your spirits."

Intrigued, I take the seat opposite Sinclair, and after a moment's silence in which he grins even more broadly, I say, "Well, come on then. What's the big news?"

"Let me say first of all that Jess is holding up well and that everyone sends their love.

"Meanwhile, the video we want to share with the court… well, last night it somehow found its way onto the World Wide Web. Apparently, it went viral in minutes. Imagine that! So, in the circumstances, there's simply no reason left to prevent us showing it in court today."

It's great news, and I can't keep the excitement from my voice. "How could that happen?" Though I have a sneaking suspicion that I already know the answer.

Sinclair continues, grinning widely, "Well, apparently someone knew that the courts always keep back-up copies of video evidence, and that someone had the code to access it and make a third copy. The weird thing is that someone else then seems to have set up a VPN to broadcast it, apparently from China! Maybe it's karma at work for the tricks the State has played on us!"

I'm smiling now, too. I smell the handiwork of Jess, Sylvie and Alex. "Any chance of tracing the leak?"

"Very unlikely," he says with a wink, then he slaps the table. "Come on, Frankie. Let's go and face the enemy!"

CHAPTER FIFTY-THREE

Zimmerman bristles when he sees Sinclair, and Longyear looks like he'd prefer to be anywhere but in court. Sinclair bounces up to the judge's bench, where Zimmerman reluctantly joins him. The conversation is short.

Longyear bangs his gavel and says, "Given last night's revelation, it's probably fair to assume that the only people in this room who have *not* seen the CCTV of Mr. Green's conversation with President Teufel are our jurors, who, as usual, were sequestered. In the circumstances, I'm forced to accept that we must correct that... We will begin today's session by playing the CCTV footage, while Mr. Sinclair continues his questioning of Mr. Green." Then he adds, his voice dripping with irritation, "Please dim the lights and let's get on with it."

Sinclair grins. "Gladly, Your Honor, but please allow me to check a couple of details with the projectionist."

Longyear replies impatiently, "You've got fifteen minutes. We will reconvene then."

***

I don't see Sinclair during the short break in proceedings, but when I'm led back up to the courtroom, he catches up with me and walks me to the dock, whispering as we move.

"Something's happened that I don't have time to explain, but it's given me an idea. What I'm thinking has never been put to the test before, but I think it's worth a shot. I certainly don't see that it can do any harm at this point."

I look across at him; there's a flintiness in his usually kind brown eyes.

"Go for it," I say as I take my seat on the witness stand.

Sinclair immediately addresses the jury, his voice loud and strong. "As Judge Longyear said before the break, I had planned to walk you through the video of my client and President Teufel's conversation on the night that President Teufel died. The short recess granted by Judge Longyear was to allow me to coordinate things with the projectionist. However, I'm sorry to tell you that two things have made that impossible."

I watch closely as Zimmerman and Longyear exchange puzzled glances. Both then lean forward, listening intently.

"Ladies and gentlemen of the jury, during his testimony you heard Mr. Zimmerman ask the Acting President about a list containing the names of foreign landowners who, Mr. Green alleges, were killed so that President Teufel could secure land for a new golf course. Those of you who saw Mr. Green's broadcast may recall that he showed that list on camera."

Most jury members nod to confirm that they had indeed seen the broadcast.

"Mr. Green claims that the Acting President dropped the list in the hangar, and when he inspected it, he discovered that he had been used, in his words, as 'The President's personal assassin.' Contrary to Mr. Green's claim, the Acting President claims that the paper was nothing more than notes on candidates for a job and that he took the paper with him when he left the hangar. So, to resolve the matter, I thought we'd start our CCTV examination with that segment of the film, so we can see with our own eyes which of them is correct."

I'm relaxed and sit back on my stool in full knowledge that my version of events will be borne out. I feel the jury's eyes on me.

Then, Zimmerman springs to his feet like a scalded cat and advances towards Sinclair, threateningly. Sinclair stands his ground.

"Both of you – over here, NOW!" Longyear bellows.

A hum of chatter descends on the courtroom as we watch the three men argue. Zimmerman pushes Sinclair, and Sinclair's fist briefly clenches at his side, although he resists the temptation to land a punch.

Finally, Longyear slumps back in his seat, looking overwhelmed, and waves them both away. Sinclair strides back to the jury, and Zimmerman paces backwards and forwards behind him, like a lion waiting to pounce.

Sinclair draws a deep breath, and shares his thoughts. "Ladies and gentlemen, please accept my apologies for what you have just witnessed. It's embarrassing and unseemly. It's just that so much has changed in our legal system since President Teufel was elected for a second time.

"As I'm sure you know, the judiciary was once a co-equal and separate branch of government. However, under President Teufel it has become more and more closely woven into the political system. We've had many laws amended on the hoof, and new laws created on the fly, to suit the ruling party's needs. Frankly, it's been hard to keep up – even for the judge!"

He pauses while a ripple of laughter subsides. I glance at the jury and am pleased to see them listening carefully, keen to discover where Sinclair is going with this line of argument

Longyear interjects sternly, "I am listening very carefully, Mr. Sinclair. Be very careful what you say next."

Sinclair glances at the judge and nods, then turns his attention back to the courtroom. Zimmerman continues to pace behind him, his face beet-red with anger.

"Several aspects of this trial have been unusual. Individually, they are not unprecedented – for example, documents have been lost in other cases, and that's happened in our case, too. Despite the piece of paper Mr. Green claims had a list of names on it being securely stored as evidence, it has now disappeared." Several jurors make a note of that fact. "And videos have been damaged in other cases. Oddly, that's happened in our case, too. I discovered in the last break in proceedings that the CCTV segment of the Acting President leaving the hangar, the very point at which Mr. Green claims the then VP dropped the list of names that we cannot now find, has been professionally cut from the tape."

I glance around the courtroom; all eyes are on Sinclair.

"And defendants do sometimes get assaulted." He points at my still-bruised face.

I try to adopt a friendly expression.

"And witnesses lie."

From the public gallery, an elderly woman's voice rings out in a loud whisper to the friend seated next to her, "Oh, he means the Acting President. Yeah, I thought he was full of it, too."

Sinclair glances up at the gallery and smiles, then slowly walks over to stand in front of the jury. "So, none of the odd things that have happened in this trial are individually strange. However, what is very strange – indeed, unprecedented – is for all of these things to happen in the same trial. But that is exactly what's happened."

Sinclair scans the room. I follow his gaze; he has everyone's attention. You could hear a pin drop.

Then, he looks at the jury's foreman. "Ladies and gentlemen of the jury, the statistical chances of all these things happening in the same trial is vanishingly small. And they prompt a question that I'd appreciate you considering: If the pattern of events is not simple misfortune, then what else could it be?"

The jury's foreman, a stout man in his mid-fifties with florid cheeks and salt-and-pepper hair in need of a trim, says without hesitation, "I guess I'd have to assume that someone is behind it, someone made these things happen…" He glances across the two rows of jurors and, encouraged by their nodding heads, adds, "Yeah, I don't see another explanation, Mr. Sinclair."

With that, Zimmerman stops prowling and strides across to the judge, his arms held wide. His tone exasperated, he says, "Your Honor, you cannot allow this. It's completely inappropriate. Stop him for God's sake!"

Longyear scans the room. The nation's press and TV cameras stare back at him, and the public gallery is hanging on Sinclair's every word. He resembles a deer caught in the headlights, indecisive and terrified. Zimmerman slaps himself on the forehead in frustration, strides back to his team and throws himself into his chair.

Sinclair resumes his slow walk as he picks up his theme again. "You are no doubt wondering where all this is leading, ladies and gentlemen of the jury, so let me assure you that I have nearly reached my destination. I would just like to share a piece of recent legal history, and the historic piece of brand-new legislation that followed." He stops by the jury's foreman again and talks to the packed courtroom – there must be a hundred people crammed into the space, all with their eyes on him. "You probably recall that when President Teufel was elected for the second time, he faced many legal problems – serious charges that could have led to prison sentences. He defended himself vigorously, claimed they were all baseless lies, nothing more than a political witch-hunt. You'll probably also recall that those cases were ultimately dismissed. Every single one of them.

"What you may not know is that in every case, a single but important piece of evidence disappeared!"

I'm not sure where Sinclair is going with his argument, but the parallel with my own case is clear, and I'm thrilled when I see several jury members nod as they make the connection. My excitement grows as I watch Zimmerman slowly walk back to his team and sit, his head in his hands.

Sinclair's continues, "What you also may not know is that, soon after his re-election, President Teufel pushed legislators to draft a new law, which was signed off by the Top Court within days. The law I'm referring to is called the Freedom Act, and it's the legal mechanism that caused all of President Teufel's charges to be dropped."

He reaches into his back pocket and extracts a single sheet of paper, folded neatly into four equal squares. He straightens it out and reads, "The Freedom Act states: Any man or woman, for whom evidence claimed by the prosecution cannot be produced in court, will be adjudged to be the victim of personal assault by the State. All charges will immediately be dropped and compensation will be calculated and paid."

Money has never been my motivating force, but freedom most definitely is. Now I see where Sinclair is leading the court; my heart races and my mouth is suddenly dry.

"President Teufel got millions as a result of applying a law that he forced lawmakers to write to ensure that he avoided trial. Think about that for a moment!"

Cries ring out from the public gallery. "Disgusting!" "Shame!" "Scum!"

I watch the TV cameras adjust their angles to film the courtroom itself.

Sinclair waits for the cries to die down, then faces the jury. "In Mr. Green's case, rather than the absence of prosecution evidence, it is evidence central to Mr. Green's ability to defend himself that has been eradicated. But the principle is plainly the same."

I watch each jury member in turn as they nod or grunt affirmation. Butterflies of excitement flutter in my stomach.

Sinclair walks to the front of the court, looks directly at the cameras and says, his voice powerful and resonant, "Quite simply, Frank Green must be freed, and all charges must be dropped. The Freedom Act demands it."

I don't know what to do, don't know how to feel. I'm excited and I long to be free, but I still don't know what will actually happen next.

The court descends into turmoil. I glance across at Zimmerman, who is yelling and pounding the judge's bench as Longyear stares feebly out at the chaos engulfing his courtroom.

After a few moments, Longyear bangs his gavel and shouts to be heard. "Court is dismissed. We will reconvene at eight am tomorrow." Few hear him above the din, and no one pays him any attention as he scurries out, slamming his chamber's door shut behind him.

CHAPTER FIFTY-FOUR

Sinclair and I don't see each other again until the next morning.

After a sleepless night, I'm weary but excited as I wait in our holding area beneath the court. Then he arrives, breathless and sweating. He pours himself a large glass of water, gulps it down and then drops into the seat opposite me.

"Just ran here, sorry for not being in touch before, it was a very long night," he says, still panting.

"No need to apologize; I know how to wait!" We both laugh gently. "I have to admit, though, I've never had nerves like this waiting on a mission. I've been tamping down the idea of freedom all night, but no matter how I squash it down it keeps bubbling up, and the thought makes my whole body tingle."

Sinclair smiles warmly. "I understand, Frankie. I very much hope that the court's decision will be to free you; I don't want to get your hopes up, but I think the stars might just be aligned!"

"That Freedom Act angle, it was pure genius!"

Sinclair blushes and looks down. "Modesty forbids me from taking the plaudits, but I am rather pleased with it." We both laugh again, a little more freely this time. "It certainly got attention, Frankie. The media have talked about nothing else, and overnight there were multiple demonstrations around the country demanding your release – demanding, too, that whoever is responsible for corrupting your trial must be tried for treason."

"Seriously?" I say, slightly surprised that so many people would take such a strong interest.

"Oh, yes, Frankie – you're a regular folk hero. Your calm and candor have really resonated with people, especially after the smoke and mirrors, lies and deception of the last decade of Teufel's rule.

"I was on all of our domestic TV networks last night giving interviews, and through the night with the international networks when they came back on air. I just finished talking to the BBC, which is why I ended up running here – I couldn't miss that one, right?!"

Laughter comes again, and I reach across the table, my hand open. "Whatever happens next, I want to thank you from the bottom of my heart for fighting for me. Honestly, I didn't know what to expect when we met, but now... I couldn't be more impressed."

Sinclair shakes my hand warmly, then we hear the call to signal that court is in session.

Excitement and fear fight for control of my mind, but as I enter the courtroom and see smiling faces everywhere, I finally relax.

***

The media presence has expanded overnight, so much so that the gallery has almost no room for anyone else. Members of the public have crowded into the lower floor and are packed tightly together. Even so, I easily spot Jess in the front row of seats, waving, and I'm thrilled to see Alex, Shirley and Sylvie with her.

The jury are seated opposite me, all staring at me intensely. They look nervous, except the colonel, who appears calm and relaxed. He glances my way, smiles briefly and nods to himself, again as if confirming an idea.

The seats allocated to Zimmerman's team are empty, and Zimmerman sits alone, looking down at the floor. Sinclair takes his seat and Judge Longyear enters. He looks like he hasn't slept and moves slowly towards his chair as if it were the gallows.

He sits for a while, shuffling papers, before he finally speaks. His tone is curt and to the point. "I will be brief. Overnight, I consulted with legal scholars and I am advised that Mr. Sinclair's interpretation of the Freedom Act is a fair one. As a result, all charges against Mr. Green are dismissed."

Cheers erupt around the courtroom. Sinclair leans back in his chair, a look of quiet satisfaction on his face, while Zimmerman quietly fumes. I can no longer restrain myself and jump up, punching the air.

Longyear bangs his gavel and waits for quiet to return. "The Freedom Act also stipulates that, once dropped, charges cannot be brought again. The Top Court is urgently reviewing the Freedom Act as we speak, but whatever their conclusion, it will apply only to future judgments."

He then addresses me directly, "Frank Green, you are free to go."

Waves of excitement wash around the court, followed by a sustained period of clapping. I stand and clap, too. I'm smiling so much it hurts!

CHAPTER FIFTY-FIVE

The next two days see a flurry of media events, and to make things easy for me to attend, Sinclair books me into a suite at the Grand Hotel – at the court's expense.

Jess and I are luxuriating in the suite's huge bed, the gentle sweat of passion drying on our bodies, when Jess looks up from my chest, props herself on her left elbow, her eyes shining, and says, "Frankie, I have to ask you something."

"Sure, anything."

"Well, the network thinks we should do another interview. To be clear, Frankie, I'm fine with whatever you feel comfortable with. I don't want to push you at all, okay? All I promised them is that I'd ask."

I laugh out loud. I don't know why it hadn't occurred to me, but it's the most obvious thing to do, especially given that first interrupted interview in the Starvation Peak studio.

***

The studio for the interview couldn't be more different than Starvation Peak. It's clean and ultra-modern, and we sit on comfortable sofas instead of plastic chairs.

The network has allocated an hour for the interview, and I gather that it will be distributed globally. Space in the schedule has been given over to an interactive chat function for people to ask their questions online. I'm out of my depth, but Jess is calm, and her calm rubs off on me.

Our conversation covers several topics that the network knows the public are curious about, including what really happened in the hangar, my arrest and what it felt like to be on trial for my life. It's cathartic to say it all out loud – without the constraints of a courtroom – and I'm grateful for the opportunity.

I'm unsure what to expect from the interactive session. I take a deep drink of water then breathe deeply while we wait for a backroom team to review the questions before sharing them with Jess, just so that she's not confronted with something offensive. But once they start, the questions come in a steady flow.

"We've had a lot of questions about your beliefs, Frankie," Jess says. "You spoke a little about that in our first broadcast together and during the trial, too, but can you tell our viewers what drives Frankie Green? What do you believe in at your very core?"

I'm never comfortable talking about myself, but I want to respect the interest people are showing in me, so I take a moment to think and then lean forward, stare into camera and let my thoughts tumble out.

"You know, in many ways, I think I'm a straightforward guy. I might have done some extraordinary things for our country, but I believe they were only possible because my core beliefs are actually pretty simple; they're what I learned growing up in Oakvale.

"I've always striven to be honest, hardworking, self-sufficient and resilient. I might get knocked down, but I will always try to get up again and work hard to stay on my feet. I've always believed that we should help those who struggle – you know, help them get back on their feet with the expectation that they will again be self-sufficient. And, of course, I believe in service. I wanted to be of service to my community as a doctor but ended up serving in the military – because I believed it was the right thing to do. I suppose, underpinning everything, I believe strongly in accountability.

"If I'm brutally honest with you now, these are the values I miss so much now in our government. The nation's tolerance of lies and self-serving corruption offends me deeply, and the fact that no one is ever bought to account sickens me."

My comments spark a flurry of follow-up questions, and for the next fifteen minutes I enjoy debating different points of view and lose myself in the conversation.

When we wrap up, Jess hugs me tight and whispers in my ear, "You were wonderful."

Everyone in the studio smiles at me and pats me on the back. It feels good.

CHAPTER FIFTY-SIX

Jess and I leave the studio about an hour later with our minds on a quiet dinner somewhere close by. It's already dark, and a light rain is falling.

As we step onto the sidewalk, I become aware of a man standing in the shadows, to the right of the studio doors. When he sees me, he immediately steps forward into the light. My training takes over – I push Jess behind me, ready to fight. But aggression gives way to confusion when I realize it's the old colonel from my trial.

"Sorry to startle you, sir," he says, holding his hands up. "I don't want to take up too much of your evening, I just want to say that I'd really appreciate the chance to talk to you about an idea that formed in my mind as your trial progressed." When I don't refuse, he relaxes a little and continues. "I'll be blunt, I think you may have exactly what this country needs to lead us out of the darkness of the Teufel era, back to the great country we used to be. I'd really appreciate the chance to pitch that idea to you, wherever and whenever you choose."

I'm stunned, speechless, but Jess whispers in my ear, "Do it."

In my mind's eye I see my mom and dad with beaming smiles; they would love the idea that the values they instilled in me could be relevant again

I shake the colonel's hand and say, "I'll look forward to it, but no promises, right?"

"Yeah, I get it, but just know," he continues, "he fooled me just as much as I believe he fooled you. I voted for him, too. But, hell, in the past we were a much better nation than he turned us into. And now he's gone, I believe we can find those values again, the values that made us special in the world – we haven't lost them, just buried them under layers of crap. With hard work we can dig them out and polish them up, become a beacon of hope in the world again, I really believe that."

I believe him, and while I don't know whether I have what it takes to successfully swap the battlefield for the ballot box, I know I'll give everything I've got to make our country great again, in the right way this time.

AUTHOR PROFILE

After an international career using data to tell business stories to the world's major automakers, Cotswolds resident Andy Turton has turned his storytelling talents to the world of fiction – *The Honourable Hitman* is his first publication.

You can find Andy at: https://www.linkedin.com/feed/

WHAT DID YOU THINK OF *THE HONORABLE HITMAN?*

A big thank you for purchasing this book. It means a lot that you chose this book specifically from such a wide range on offer. I do hope you enjoyed it.

Book reviews are incredibly important for an author. All feedback helps them improve their writing for future projects and for developing this edition. If you are able to spare a few minutes to post a review on Amazon, that would be much appreciated.

PUBLISHER INFORMATION

Rowanvale Books provides publishing services to independent authors, writers and poets all over the globe. We deliver a personal, honest and efficient service that allows authors to see their work published, while remaining in control of the process and retaining their creativity. By making publishing services available to authors in a cost-effective and ethical way, we at Rowanvale Books hope to ensure that the local, national and international community benefits from a steady stream of good quality literature.

For more information about us, our authors or our publications, please get in touch.

www.rowanvalebooks.com
info@rowanvalebooks.com

www.ingramcontent.com/pod-product-compliance
Lightning Source LLC
Chambersburg PA
CBHW020411210626
46816CB00006BB/2232